The Sun and The Moon

The King

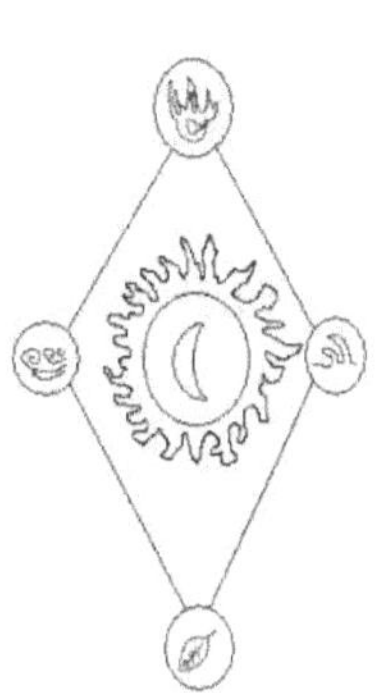

A CIP catalogue record for this book is available from the British Library.

Published by Creative Publications
www.creative-publications.co.uk

ISBN: 9781916208704

THE KING

CHAPTER ONE

My eyes flickered open.

I had woken up and it was pitch black. It was so dark I wondered if my eyes were really open. *Where am I?* I thought. *What was I was trapped in*? It was cramped and I could barely move.

"Oh my god I'm in my bloody coffin. Don't. Panic." 30 seconds later I was in full panic mode. "HELP, HELP I'M IN HERE!" I shouted, until my throat was raw.

"Ok Felix, think, how am I going to get out of this?" I took a few deep breaths to calm myself down; then I used my earth possession and pulled the dirt from underneath the coffin, which in turn pushed the coffin above ground. I pushed the lid with all my strength and it suddenly flew open. I quickly crawled out and laid my face down in the grass.

It was dark outside, and the moon was above the trees, I rolled onto my back, looking up at the stars. I was so happy I couldn't help but cry; I let it all out, you know, like a slobbering mess. Once finished, I pulled myself together. *What do I do now?* I thought, I couldn't exactly go, home, could I? Everyone thinks I'm dead. The only person I could go to is Sean. He would be the one person who would be less likely to freak out. I got to my feet and felt a bit uneasy on them. I stood for a second to catch my bearings.

As I walked out of the graveyard, I started to worry that I was going to scare the life out of him when he saw me. It only took a few minutes to walk to Sean's house as he only lived three blocks away.

Once I got to his house, I saw all the lights were out apart from his. *Thank god* I thought. I felt relieved. I know this is a movie cliché, but I found some stones and threw them, one by one, at the window until he opened it. I couldn't think of another way to get his attention. I stayed in the dark as much as I could, so he couldn't see all of me. "Who's that?" he called.

"Me," I tried to sound like Karl. "Is that you Karl?" he replied.

"Yeah, come down," I replied. "Ok, I will be there in a sec."

I started pacing back and forth, thinking: *He's going to freak out... no, this is Sean, he won't, he will be fine.*

"Karl," Sean whispered as he shut the door.

"Sean, please don't freak out," I whispered.

"Who is that? You're not Karl," Sean said, getting closer.

"Sean, it's me, Felix," I said, as I walked out into the moonlight.

Sean just stopped in his tracks.

"Sean, please don't freak out," I repeated.

"Why would I freak out?" he responded. "It's just that one of my best friends, that's been dead for over a year, is standing in front of me. No, no freaking out here, I must be dreaming" Sean said, as he turned to go back into the house.

"Sean, wait." He turned back to me; I could see tears running down his face. "how long have I been gone for? Can't be more than a few months?"

"One year, seven months more like, give or take a few days," he replied, while whipping his tears away with his sleeve.

"Sean, sorry, but this is not a dream." He turned around and started walking back towards the house. "Sean please, it's not a dream I'm really here!" I exclaimed, grabbing his arm tightly.

"Ouch" he said, spinning around. "That hurt!"

"See you're not asleep and I am really here."

"Felix!" I just nodded, then he launched and gave me the biggest of hugs. I hugged him back so hard, he is one of my best friends; and I've missed him so much I never wanted to let him go.

"Where have you been? How are you still alive? We buried you, who else knows?"

Here comes the barrage of questions, but I was ready for them. I knew he would have loads to ask. He pulled away and walked towards the kerb outside of his house. We both sat down, and I answered each question, one by one. It started to get light out by the time I had finished telling him everything about where I had been and what had happened.

"I can't believe it's been nearly seven years in your timeline. So, that makes you what, 22 nearly 23? But you still only look 16. Well, your 17now, because you missed your birthday," Sean said.

"Do I really only look 16?" I asked. I haven't looked at myself, there wasn't a mirror in my coffin when I woke," I joked.

Sean chuckled. "Ok, so what do we do now?"

"I really don't know Sean. I can't just go home and walk in like nothing's happened…I've been gone for a long time, nearly two years your telling me"

"I know, but what about if I get everyone here?" he sounded excited; as though we were planning a party for everyone to welcome me back from the afterlife.

"That could work, but what about your parents?" I asked. "Why don't we go to Drake Forest?"

"NO, no one has been back there since it happened."

"What did you tell everyone about what happened to me?" I asked, but I could tell he didn't want to talk about it. "It's ok, you don't need to tell me, I'm sure I will find out in time. So, where are we going to do this?".

"Here, my Dad is never home," Sean gestured toward his parent's house.

"What about your Mum?" I asked.

"She passed away 3 months after you," he replied quietly.

"Oh, Sean, I'm so sorry."

"It was a car accident. She drove off the embankment at Widow's Peak. We think she had some mental issues, because she went missing a few weeks before. My Dad looked for her, but then he got a call saying they found someone but couldn't identify them. After they completed tests and checked her dental records, they confirmed it was her.

I was in shock. Mrs Hardy was a lovely woman; she always made my favourite dinner whenever I stayed around.

"Ok, when shall we do this?" I asked, trying to change the subject, as I could see Sean was getting distressed.

"Erm, we can do it today. My Dad is working in the next town over, so he won't be back till late. Let's get you in the house so no one sees you and you can get changed. You look like you're going to a funeral."

"Ha-ha, very funny."

CHAPTER TWO

Once I was up in Sean's room, I changed into some of his clothes, but I was a good foot taller than him, so all of his trousers were jack ups. We waited until his Dad left for work then Sean grabbed me a pair of his Dad's trousers. They fit me better than Sean's did.

I pulled on a hoodie with a picture of a zombie on, a huge Zombie, with guts coming out of its stomach. "Really Sean, a zombie?"

"What, it was the first one I picked up," he said defensively.

"Yeah right, how are you going to get everyone here anyway?" I asked, pulling the hood up over my head. "I'm going to text them," Sean said, giving me a strange look.

I've been stuck in Alicade for nearly seven years and they had no phones, no internet, nothing. "I'm texting 'ditch school and come here, I've got something epic to show you', I think that will work," Sean said, looking pleased with himself. "Who have you texted?"

"Everyone: Karl, Star, Chadwick, Ben and Red," he counted them off on his fingers.

Just at the mention of Star's name I could have cried, the tears stung my eyes. But I was a grown man...well in my head I was.

Sean's phone was going mad with texts, so I just left him to it. I stood next to the window looking out. Everyone was going about their day like they normally do, going to work, school or taking their dog for a walk. How could all this normal stuff be happening when my return from the dead was going to shock so many people; and change everything in their lives? "Ok, it's set. Star is going to pick everyone up. They should be here around 10. Felix are you ok?" he asked.

I had gone into a trance looking at everyone outside.

"It's just strange being back here in my old life after what I've seen, it's like it never happened."

"Erm, well, I can't even comprehend what happened to you there, but when we all get together, we can talk through it all." I just nodded, still looking out of the window.

It was just before 10 when Sean told me to go into the spare room.

"Wait here until I come and get you," he instructed. "Ok," I replied.

I sat on the bed with my head resting on the wall. I could hear muffled talking next door. I put my ear up against the wall and closed my eyes, trying to concentrate on what they were saying. Suddenly, Sean burst through the door and scared the crap out of me.

"It's time," he said.

"What do they know?" I whispered. "They know I want to show them something," Sean said, leading me out of the room. He stopped just before his doorway. "Ok, just wait there."

So, I just stood there, waiting to the right of the door so no one could see me from inside the room.

"Ok everyone, what I've got to show you is just outside. But, before I show you, you need to keep an open mind."

"Just get on with it," Chadwick said, getting mad.

"All right, you can come in now," Sean called.

I knew that was my cue, so I stepped to the side and walked into the room.

Silence… no one spoke for ages.

"Hello…" I couldn't think of anything else to say. Still nothing, so I just stood there waiting.

"Look guys, its Felix, he's back," Sean said. "Well we can bloody see that can't we, but how?" Chadwick asked, moving closer.

"Can someone die and come back?" I tried to joke, but it went down like a led balloon.

Chadwick poked my arm as though I would disappear into thin air. "He's real," he said to the others behind him. "Did you think I was a fake, or a ghost or something" I questioned. "Felix is that really you?" whispered Karl, moving closer.

I just nodded. Suddenly, Karl pushed Chadwick out of the way and threw himself at me. He held onto me so tight and began to cry.

My poor, sensitive Karl, I thought.

Ben and Red came over to see if I was real as well, but Star just stayed at the back of the room. She didn't move an inch.

I will tell you the truth. It hurt me that she stayed away.

We all sat down, and I told them everything. Karl sat next to me, so close he just kept touching my arm. I think he thought that I was going to disappear if he let go. They told me that they had told everyone that we were all climbing trees (yes, I know, climbing trees at our age) and I slipped and fell. That they had tried, but they couldn't revive me.

I was glad they all stuck together while I was gone. They all asked me questions apart from Star; she was still at the other side of the room.

"Star, aren't you going to say something? You've been pining over him," said Chadwick.

"I can't do this," she said; then she was gone. She had teleported away. "STAR, I was only joking!" Chadwick said out loud.

"Well, it wasn't very nice was it," said Karl. He was handling it all a lot better than I'd thought he would.

"It's ok. It's probably too much to take in all at once. She will come around, I hope," I said.

"What's going to happen now?" said Red. "Your guess is as good as mine," I answered. "What about Dad?" Ben said. "We can't tell him."

"Why? He knows everything now. We told him the truth about everything," said Red.

I put my hands over my face in disbelief. "How could you tell him?"

"You didn't see him after you died, Felix. He was a wreck, not opening the store, not getting out of bed for days. So, we told him, but we didn't tell him about Chadwick and Star," Ben said, standing up. "And how is he now that he knows?"

"Much better, the day after we told him it was like he was himself again," said Red.

"I think they're right, we should tell him, he needs to know," said Sean.

"Ok let's do it," I said, with no confidence at all.

So, I stayed with Sean and Karl while the Satan twins went and got our Dad; and Chadwick went to talk to Star.

Walking down the stairs, I could hear my Dad saying, "This had better be good; I closed the store for this."

I walked down the rest of the stairs and stood in the living room doorway. "Dad," I said, but it came out as a whisper.

He quickly spun around. *I'd missed his big, manly face*, I thought to myself.

I walked to him as he just stood there staring, I smiled at him. "Hello, Dad."

"Felix, FELIX!" he threw his arms around me and held on to me so tightly I couldn't breathe. How funny would that be if I died again after just coming back? "Dad. I. Can't. Breathe." I gasped.

"Sorry. I just can't believe you're here," he said, pulling away. And so, for the third time today, I told my story.

"Wow…it's just so unbelievable," said Phil. "It sounds crazy I know, but it happened. I was made an offer to be head of the guards. I was really tempted to take it, but I've got so much going on here that I wanted to come back. How's Mum and Freddy?" I said.

I nearly choked on Freddy's name. I'm pretty sure Star is the only one who knows how protective I was over him before I cured him of his cancer.

"Your Mother was really depressed for a while, now she is just coping, and Freddy asks about you every day. He even sleeps in your room at night when he's having a really bad night. It calms him down," Dad explained.

Red and Ben nodded in agreement, "He's been unwell for a few weeks, and he's really been pining after you."

"What do you mean by 'he's been unwell'?" I asked, my heart sinking with dread.

"He went for some tests last week and we should get the results any day now," said Red.

I put my face in my hands.

"No, this can't be happening again," I groaned.

"What Felix? What can't be happening again?" asked Dad, concerned.

"Freddy has leukemia. Well, had. I helped cure it. Well, I thought I had anyway," I was on the verge of tears.

"It's not leukemia, that test was negative; as were all the other 'biggie's'. It's not leukemia or any cancers. They're just unsure what it is. How did you help cure him, Felix? Why didn't you tell us he was poorly?" said Dad, getting a little mad that he was only finding this out now.

"I'm a very special avatar, Dad. I have the power of energy, so I gave him some to help fight it off himself," I explained. "I want to see him."

"Felix you can't, you're dead."

"The hell I can't, look at me Dad. Do I look dead? This is my body, my own!" I shouted, storming upstairs to cool off.

I really have to see him, I thought.

"I'm going to see him," I said out loud. I walked into Sean's room and opened the window. I don't know what came over me. I couldn't help but jump out of his window without even thinking. I landed on a pillow of air which broke my fall and jumped over the 6-ft fence. The almost seven years I'd spent in Alicade has done me some good. I can now control my powers and do all these crazy stunts.

I ran as fast as I could to my house. I didn't care if anyone saw me; all I could think about was Freddy.

Once I reached my house I snuck in the back gate and made my way through the bushes to the window. I moved slowly so I could peak through the window. There he was, just sitting there at his little blue table, staring into space.

I had mixed emotions upon seeing Freddy. On the one hand, I was happy because he was just there in front of me and I could see that he was ok. On the other, I was worried about the test's Dad had told me about; and what they might reveal.

"Felix," said a voice behind me.

I spun around and saw Star standing to the side of the window.

"Star," I said, taking a step closer; but she took a step back.

"Felix, what are you doing here?"

"I wanted to see Freddy."

"Well, you've seen him now, so you should leave," Star said in an annoyed tone. "Star, why do you sound so cold?" I asked, hurt.

"Oh, I don't know. Maybe because you're meant to be dead, but yet here you are standing in front of me. I mourned you Felix. I mourned you for months," Star said, hitting my chest with her fists, hitting me again and again.

I grabbed her arms as she went to hit me for the fourth time, and I pulled her close. She tried to pull away from me, but I put both arms around her and held on so tight. Suddenly, she burst into tears. We stood there for what felt like hours, I let her get all her frustration and anger out.

Once she stopped crying, I loosened my grip.

"Felix, I can't believe you're back, I've missed you so much!"

I noticed her hair was turning red, so I took some of the energy away as I spoke.

"I've missed you too."

We moved away from the window when I noticed my Mum, Sue, was coming closer to it. She was cleaning an already spotless house.

"Since I've been gone, what have you been up to?" I asked Star.

"Nothing. I tried to help Chadwick with his ability, but my magic couldn't help him."

"I'm not surprised. You would need to use my energy possession to get Chadwick's foresight back, not magic. That's why you couldn't help," I replied.

"I never thought of it that way. I've tried to find out what's wrong with Freddy, but I just can't figure out what it is," she said, with a concerned look on her face.

"My Father said something like that; that Freddy has been going for some tests."

"He's not sick Felix, not like before, it's different. It's like he's here and not here, all at the same time. It's like there's something missing."

I was confused. 'Missing', what did she mean by that?

"I need to see him," I said.

"Not now, wait until tonight then I will take you to him," she replied.

"Ok, can you take me back to Sean's house? They're bound to have noticed that I've gone."

In a flash, we were gone.

CHAPTER THREE

Later that night Star took me to Freddy while he was sleeping, he looked so peaceful and still.

I gently put my hand on his. The energy he was giving off was strange. It didn't feel the same as leukemia, but I knew I had felt this kind of energy before. I just couldn't put my finger on where or when.

"Star, I know now what you meant when you said there was something different about Freddy," I whispered as we left his room; and snuck into my old bedroom.

Nothing in the room had changed apart from the clothes that were usually on the floor had been put away.

"What did you feel?" she asked.

"It's strange. I've felt the same thing before, but I just don't know where though," I said, sitting on my bed.

"Could it have been when you were de.... in Alicade?"

"Maybe, I just can't think," I put my head in my hands, trying to think straight.

"Maybe you should rest for a while, you've had a long and emotional day," Star suggested gently.

"Maybe you're right, Star," I said, laying down on my bed. I had forgotten just how comfy my bed was.

Star laid down beside me. She kissed my forehead, and then I was fast asleep.

When I woke up, it felt like I had never left.

Star must have left during the night. I got up in my old surroundings and just went on autopilot. I went to the bathroom that was joined to my room. I showered, brushed my hair and teeth and dressed in joggers and a hoody.

Walking into the kitchen my Mum, Sue, said, "Morning Felix, honey, you hungry?"

"Starving, Mum," I said unthinkingly.

There was silence, followed by a crash. I turned and saw that a plate had smashed on the floor. Mum slowly turned around; she was white as a sheet.

Oh my god, Felix, you're a bloody doughnut, everyone thinks you're dead, I thought to myself.

"Mum let me explain," I pleaded.

Before I could say another word, a cup went flying past my face and hit the wall behind me, then another.

"Get out of here, you're an imposter!" she screamed. Then she started on the utensils, they came hurtling towards me too.

"Mum, please, just listen to me please."

"GET OUT!" she shouted.

"Ok, ok I'm going," I said.

Backing out of the kitchen, towards the front door, I quickly left the house.

I didn't know where to go. I had no shoes on. I started walking towards Sean's house, but he wasn't there. *Crap they're at school, where am I going to go now? Dad*, I thought.

So, I went to the hardware store. I had to cover my face as I walked down to the town as, technically, I was dead. I didn't want the whole town freaked out by seeing me.

I reached the store and peeked through the window to see if there was anyone inside. I ran in the door and turned the sign to closed.

"God, that was close," I said, trying to get as far away from the windows and doors as I could.

"Can I help...Felix what are you doing here?" Dad asked.

"Oh, Dad, I've screwed up big time."

"What is it?" he asked, walking over to the door and locking it.

"Well, I kind of forgot that I should be dead, and I walked into the kitchen and spoke to Mum."

The shock on his face told me I was in trouble.

"Dad, say something."

"FELIX YOU STUPID BOY, I TOLD YOU NOT TO GO TO THE HOUSE!" he roared.

"I know, I'm sorry; it's just I slept in my own bed and waking up in my room, it just felt like a crazy dream".

"What am I going to do?" Dad said, putting his arms around me.

"Sorry, Dad."

"It's ok son, you just stay here, and I will go see if she's ok, lock the door behind me."

"OK, will do. Oh, and Dad, while you're there, can you get me some shoes?"

He ruffled my hair and said, "Will do, don't forget to lock the door when I leave. Try and stay out of view of the window."

I just nodded then he left.

I locked the door as he said and went to the back of the store to the till and sat down behind it.

Hours ticked by and I was getting really bored, there's only so many times you can count the nails in the box under the till. I stood them up on their ends in a line. I laid them back in the box, one row with the heads up the top and one row with the heads at the bottom. There were 656 nails to be exact, I counted.

I was just about to count them again when there was a knock at the door. I froze. *What do I do?* I thought.

I slowly got up on my knees to look over the counter. I could see two people outside. One was looking in the shop and the other one was behind the first. "If I just stay quiet, they will leave," I said to myself.

"Felix," one said through the letterbox.

"Sean, is that you?"

"Yes, now open the door."

I quickly got up and opened the door for them. I hugged them both in turn as they entered the store. I locked the door behind them and moved them to the back.

"How did you know I was here?" I asked.

"Your Father said you needed these?" Karl said, pulling my black Converse trainers out of his bag. I put them on straight away as my feet were getting cold.

"I don't suppose you have any food in there was well? I'm starving."

They both shook their heads.

"No, but I will go get you something if you want?"

"Oh, would you Karl, I haven't eaten since I've been back."

"What do you want?" he asked. "Food. Just any food"

"Alright, I'll be back," Karl laughed, as he opened the door and left.

Sean and I were talking while waiting for Karl to get back with the food when the door dinged open.

"About time Karl," Sean said. "Oh. Hello, Mrs. Carter." Sean waved his hand to me to scoot up under the till.

"Hello, Sean. I didn't know you worked here?"

"Err well, err, I'm just helping Mr. Moon out for half an hour"

"That's nice of you. It's such a shame his boy died so young."

I rolled my eyes. I thought about popping out from under the counter and scaring the crap out of her. Now, that would be funny, just to even think of it. I had to cover my mouth, so I didn't laugh out loud.

Sean kicked me and said, "How can I help you, Mrs. Carter?"

"Well, I'm after an, oh, what's it called? You can tighten things with it and adjust the size. Oh, what's it called?"

"Wrench," I tried to whisper, but Sean was just not getting it.

"Sorry, Mrs. Carter, I don't know what you are after," he said. She mumbled something else.

I thought *I know what I can do.* I quickly peeked up from the counter and used my wind power to knock a wrench off the shelf.

"Oh, what was that?" said Mrs. Crater, making her jump.

Sean quickly moved to where the noise came from.

"That's what I'm looking for? a wrench."

At that moment, Karl burst through the door saying, "Food's here...oh, sorry Mrs. Carter."

"That's OK. Here you go, laddie...keep the change," she said and then left.

"Lock the door, Karl. Sean, you are so stupid sometimes. Wrench, how the hell didn't you know what that was?" I joked.

"Hey Felix, look what else I brought" Karl said excitedly.

He pulled a black hair die out of his bag, "what's that for" Sean said before I could.

"To die hair you idiot, I just thought that as Felix is meant to be dead, he could use it"

 "You know what that's not a bad idea, thanks Karl" I said taking the black hair die off him, black hair? *I could never imagine myself with different colour hair.*

We sat there talking...well they talked, and I stuffed my face full of pizza and fries. It was Karl's idea, so I told him that he had to die my hair, I have to admit, I do look a lot better with black hair than I did dirty blond.

It was gone 10pm and Dad hadn't come back. Sean and Karl had left hours ago, and I had started counting the nails again, when the door opened. I knew I locked it after my friends had left, so I looked over the counter and my heart stopped. It was Kayos. Our last meeting didn't end so well.

"Felix, I know you're there."

I stood up, feeling so scared, but then I thought: *I'm not the same person I was, I'm a mod avatar for Christ sake!*

"What do *you* want?" I asked angrily.

"Felix you look very different with black hair, I don't like it"

"Who cares what you like or not, WHAT DO YOU WANT?" I shouted.

Kayos held his hands up and said, "I'm not here to fight, just to talk."

"Go on then, talk".

Kayos was slowly making his way to where I was standing.

"I was thinking that we should talk, you and I," he said.

"Talk about what? The fact that your evil."

"Ouch Felix, that hurt my feelings," he replied sarcastically.

"I've got a sense that I'm not the only evil one here. I'm the same as Star you know. I can feel that you're different too."

"I am different. I'm an avatar."

"Oh no, Felix, you're more than a normal avatar, you're special," Kayos said, with a glint in his eye.

"And what has it got to do with you?". "I just thought I would talk to you."

"About what?" I was getting nervous, as he was within arm's reach of me, so I was getting ready to fight.

"What was it like being dead? What did you do on the other side?"

He knew full well what I had done when I was dead as he had been there too. "I went into the light. Then I woke up in my coffin. Kayos, you know what happened, you broke bloody the portal and watched when I kicked your army's butt. You were a big old chicken and didn't fight!"

"Careful what you say, boy," Kayos said, clenching his fists.

"No, I won't watch what I say, this is my family's business and if you don't like what I say, you know where the door is."

I could see in Kayos face he didn't get spoken to like this very often. "Look here –" he began.

"What's going on here and what have you done to your hair?" Dad quizzed touching my hair after returning back.

"It was Karl's idea; don't you like it?".

"Yes, it's nice but who was that person?"

"Nothing Dad, he was just leaving. Weren't you?"

"Yes, I was, until next time, Felix," then just he just vanished.

"What was that all about?" Dad asked.

"Well Dad, that was Annadora's son, Kayos"

"I didn't know she had any kids."

"Yeah well, she has three, but you don't need to worry about them, just Kayos."

"Felix, do you know who they are?"

"Yes, but they're on my side." I replied.

"I don't know about that Felix, it sounds dodgy to me. I think you should stay away from them, just to be on the safe side."

"It's OK Dad, I know what I'm doing ...anyway, how's Mum?"

"Well, when I got home, she was crying, but I calmed her down and told her everything. She thought I was crazy, but she's waiting at home to see you," he explained.

"Is she really OK with all this craziness?" I said.

"Come on son, let's go home."

We left the shop.

CHAPTER FOUR

O nce we got home, Dad went into the house first; and I could just about hear them talking when Star appeared beside me, making me jump. "Oh, crap Star! I'm definitely getting you a bell to wear." I exclaimed. "Felix, stop exaggerating. Why are you waiting out here?" she asked.

"My Dad's told my Mum what's going on with me and everything else. Star, how did you know that I was out here?"

"Well...I've kind of put a spell around the house so that when someone, or something, breaks the circle, I get a pulse of energy. Then, I come over and look," Star said, feeling a little guilty.

"Thanks Star, for looking after my family," I said, hugging her. Then I kissed her on the cheek, then on the lips.

We were in full make-out mode. I pulled her closer. I could feel her energy flow through me, when we were interrupted by someone clearing their throat.

We quickly stepped away from each other. It was my parents standing at the door.

"Mum." "Felix," she said, holding her arms out. I ran into them without any hesitation. "Oh Felix, I've missed you so much!"

"And I've missed you too, Mum," I said, hugging her tighter.

"I'll see you tomorrow after school, Felix and I like the hair,"
Star said, walking away, but I knew she would be in my room
later.

Mum and I walked into the living room, and I told her my story. I
showed her what I can do. I formed a wind, water, and fire orb,
letting them just float in mid-air.

"I won't use energy or earth, because, if I use them: firstly, I
would wake everyone up; and, secondly, I don't use the energy
one too much. It's a scary power to have if used incorrectly. It
hurts people and I don't think you would like it if I pulled all your
energy out of you."

They both shook their heads.

"So, you're back for good?" Mum said, still red-eyed.

"I am, well until I'm old and decrepit." I joked.

"OK Felix, I think it's bedtime," said Dad, getting up off the sofa.

"Good night Mum, Dad," I said, then I started for the stairs.

I turned back to see my parents hugging, with Mum saying,

"I can't believe he's back, I'm so happy!"

That put a huge smile on my face.

Walking into my room, I closed the door behind me.

"Star?" I whispered. No answer. "Star, I know you're there, I can
feel you."

"Where am I, then?"

I stood in the middle of my room and closed my eyes. I could feel where she was, which was straight behind me, so I quickly spun around and grabbed her.

"There you are," I laughed.

"Well done, you are very good at the energy power now."

"Yeah well, I worked with a man called Kava and he was amazing. He taught me so much about fighting and about the balance of powers; and you will never guess how old he was?"

"I don't know, 34."

"Try 398. Time works so differently there. They did try and explain it to me, but I just didn't get it.

"So, you going to tell me about the hair?"

"It was Karl's idea, but I don't think I'm going to keep it as my Mum just told me I look like Red and Ben".

"You look nothing like them, I really like it" Star said running her hands through my hair".

Anyway, I had a little visitor at the store earlier."

"Who?" Star asked.

"Kayos. Even after all the crap that's happened between him and I, every time I see him it strikes fear through me." "What did he want?"

"Just to talk, but we didn't really talk about much."

"Well, that was then; and this is now," Star said, kissing me on the lips. "I could get used to this," I said, smiling.

We kissed again; we kissed for so long we had to stop for air.

"I think It's time for me to go," said Star.

"But you normally stay with me at night?" I said, not wanting her
to leave. "I know, but now that we have kissed, I don't
think it's right," "What do you think I'm going to do? I'm still the
same me."

"I know, but still. See you tomorrow," Star said, kissing me gently
on the lips. "Good night," I whispered. "Good night, Felix," then
she was gone.

I went to bed happy, as it only took me dying for my feelings for
Star to show, but now I know what Granddad Felix was talking
about when he said she was 'the one'. I was still unsure if I was
going to tell her about that just yet. I fell into a dreamless sleep,
willing it to be tomorrow already.

CHAPTER FIVE

In the morning I went down for breakfast, knowing that my Mum had already taken Freddy to nursery.

"Morning Felix, you hungry?" she asked, as I walked into the kitchen.

I put my arms up in defence, "You're not going to throw stuff at me again, are you?"

"Oh Felix, just sit down before I change my mind."

So, I sat down as she put a plate in front of me with scrambled eggs, bacon, sausage and beans. "Thanks Mum," I said.

Mum sat down at the table with me and I could sense she wanted to say something but didn't know how say it.

"Mum, whatever it is, you can ask me," I said, putting some eggs in my mouth.

"Your Dad said that you helped Freddy once when he was sick, how exactly did you help him?" she asked.

I put my fork down and said, "Well, at first I didn't know what I was doing, until someone told me what I was doing –"

"Who told you?" she interrupted.

"Well, I'm not sure I can disclose my sources until I've spoken to them."

Mum nodded, "OK, carry on."

"It was my energy power that was helping him fight leukemia off," I continued, to which she began to cry. *Oh, crap,* I thought. "It's OK Mum, he's better. There's no trace of leukemia in his system."

"Felix, what's wrong with him now? He's not the same", she said, still sobbing.

"I don't know Mum, but we will find out. His energy feels different and I can't put my finger on it. It's like he's there, but he's not alone."

Then it hit me like a wrecking ball. When I was in Alicade, Kayos possessed one of the guards there; and was getting inside information about us, until I stumbled upon what he was doing by mistake. I regularly gave the guards energy boosts while we were fighting, but this time it bounced off a guard and threw me across the room, knocking me out. Kava had told me later that this particular guard, Reid, was possessed and that it took three of the most powerful witches Alicade had to exorcise Kayos from his body.

Unfortunately, Kayos left his calling card of death before he departed. Reid had died as a result of the exorcism because when Kayos left his body, he took Reid's energy and power with him.

I was knocked out so I couldn't help him. It took years for me to get over it, as I thought it was my fault; and I blamed myself for

Reid's death. Kava helped me through it, telling me that

possessing someone was an ancient tactic that no one had used

for centuries. One of the witches told me that there is no way to

save a possessed host. Their energy and power get's combined

and when they're exorcised the host loses everything, including

their life.

But in the back of my mind, I knew I could save him because I

possess the energy power, but it was too late, he was dead, and

even I can't bring people back to life.

"FELIX!" My Mum, shouting my name, brought me back to reality.

"Sorry Mum, I just spaced out for a second," I said, shaking my

head.

"What were you thinking about?"

"When I was in Alicade, something happened and I think it might

be connected to Freddy, but I need to talk to someone to be

sure."

"Is there anything I can do to help?" she asked.

"No, not unless you're a witch in your spare time?" I joked.

"No, sorry," she said, looking helpless.

"I didn't think you were. It's OK. I'll have a chat with the gang."

"Felix, who else knows you're alive?"

"Well, there's you; Dad; Star; her brother Chadwick; Sean; Karl

and the Satan twins. I didn't really want you involved in all of this.

Dad was only just in the loop, he doesn't know about everything that's going on," I answered.

"Well, I'm in, whether you like it or not."

I was impressed with my Mum's determination. "OK, well Freddy can't know I'm back yet, so keep him occupied until I've figured this out completely." I warned her.

"OK Felix, how long do you need?" she said.

"A few days maybe," I replied.

"That's fine. I'll go and stay at Jane and Ken's for a while," Mum said, getting up from her chair.

"It's going to be OK, Mum. I promise, I'll give everything I have to see Freddy well again, whatever it takes."

She nodded and left the kitchen.

I finished my breakfast and decided to make my way to my room, but halfway up the stairs I could hear voices coming from my room.

I quietly snuck to my door. I could feel multiple energy signatures coming from my room. They belonged to Sean, Karl and Star. Walking through the door, I saw that Sean and Karl had already set up the Xbox and were playing a racing game.

"Hey, Felix. Just like old times," Karl said.

"Well, apart from you're meant to be in the cafeteria, not being transported to my bedroom by Star," I quipped.

"And you're meant to be dead, so get over it," he joked back.

I couldn't stop myself laughing, as he was right. "OK, now that I've got most of the gang here, I think I might know what's wrong with Freddy. I think he is possessed," I said, Star standing silent, while Sean and Karl laughed.

"Stop laughing, it's true. The more I think about it, the more I think I'm right." Then I told them the story that I'd just told Mum, about the dead guard, Reid, from Alicade. "Star, do you think Kayos could be doing this to Freddy?" I asked.

"Yes, he could be, but if he was stuck there with you, then he can't be the one possessing Freddy. It has to be…"

Annadora.

We all knew the answer, but no one said it aloud. "So, how are we going to save Freddy?" I asked.

"Felix, there's no cure for possession, not for the host," Star replied softly.

"A witch in Alicade said that the host's power and energy get intertwined with their controller's, but what if I give my energy to Freddy to help him fight it?"

"Can you do that?" said Sean.

"I don't know, but I can practice on you guys."

So, I tried to shift my powers to another person.

I know I can give someone more power if they already have that power but giving power to someone that hasn't got *any powers at all…* well, that would be tricky. But I know it's possible.

Star, Sean and Karl never went back to school that day, or even for the rest of the week. They stayed around my house.

By the weekend, I'd successfully given my wind ability to Sean– Karl freaked out when I tried with him. I didn't try with Star. Because she's a witch, she already has supernatural abilities; so, it would be too easy to push my power to her.

"So, Sean, how does it feel?" I asked.

"It feels like there's a whirlwind in my body. I can *feel it*, it's crazy!" Sean said, trying his new power out by forming a wind orb in his hands.

"Felix, try and use the wind power," Star said.

I tried to lift my bedside lamp with the wind power and the force of it hit me like a giant elastic band. It sent me flying across the room.

"Felix, are you OK?" asked Star.

"Ouch," I grunted in reply, my whole-body tingling.

"What happened?" Karl said, helping me up.

"He's got his wind power back. The whirlwind inside me has gone," Sean said.

"Well, at least we know that you can get it back," Star joked.

"Now I know how to do it, shall we try my energy power now?" I asked excitedly.

Hours ticked by, but I just couldn't shift the energy power out of me. I even tried to give it to Star, but still nothing.

"Why isn't this working?" I shouted, frustrated. "I'm doing everything the same."

"It's OK, Felix," Sean said.

"No Sean, it's not OK. I need to do this for Freddy, if I can't do this, he's dead."

"Erm Felix, I've been thinking, I don't think this is going to work," said Karl, who was sitting on the window ledge, looking down at his entwined fingers.

"What do you mean Karl? And it better be good. This is my little brother's life we are talking about."

"Well, erm...you know when you told us about the time you spent in Alicade? Well, you told us about that soldier, that you gave him a boost and you got kicked back and knocked out. Well...isn't this the same as then, you giving your energy to a possessed person?" Everyone sat in silence for what felt like an eternity. We all knew Karl was right, but I just couldn't bring myself to admit it; so, I just stormed out of my room, ran down the stairs three at a time and out the front door, not caring who saw me (don't forget I'm meant to be dead).

I could hear Star, Sean and Karl shouting after me, "Felix, wait!"

"No, leave me alone!"

I turned, and with all the wind power I could muster, I threw them away from me. I instantly regretted it. Star was the only one that saved herself from hitting the floor, but Sean and Karl hit the floor hard; hitting their heads on the concrete.

My heart sank and I felt disgusted with myself. "What have I done?" I said aloud, looking down at my shaking hands.

Star went running over to the person closest to her. "FELIX, HELP ME!" she shouted, but my feet just wouldn't move. "FELIX!" Star shouted louder.

"Sorry," I whispered, as I turned and ran towards Drake Forest. I know running away was really bad and a childish thing to do, but I've just hurt two of the most important people in my life. I walked around Drake Forest for hours, until I come across my burial site, where I got my earth possession. I sat next to the hole and just stared in. So much has happened since I was last here, alive that is.

The only person I needed to talk to was Granddad Felix, but there's only one problem: I don't know how to get back to the white room. Granddad Felix had told me I could go back any time I wanted now that the portal was fixed, but he didn't tell me how. So, I just sat there with my eyes closed, thinking about the white room, the crystal city of Alicade and the huge shard of crystal that the castle is made of. Then my head started spinning and my breathing slowed. My head spun slowly at first then the spinning got faster and faster, until everything went black.

CHAPTER SIX

I woke up in the white room.

"Granddad Felix," I shouted, as loud as I could. I shouted until my throat was dry and sore. Granddad Felix never showed up. I sat down in a corner of the room, with my knees up to my chest and cried into my hands.

I just thought, *I've been crying a lot lately; and there's more to come, I'm sure.*

I don't know how much time passed: 10 minutes, one hour, maybe two. I stayed there until something touched the top of my head. Looking up with blurry eyes, I could just about make out the very person I'd come to see.

"Granddad Felix," I crocked out, a little louder than a whisper.

"Felix my boy, what on earth is the matter?"

"Granddad, I've messed up. I've messed up really bad," I said, crying (again).

Granddad Felix knelt in front of me and said, "Tell me what happened?"

So, I spilled my guts to him and told him everything about Freddy being possessed and using my powers on Star, Sean and Karl.

"Granddad...I think I'm losing the fight. Please, help me."

"Come with me, my boy and we will figure this out," he said; and, in a blinding light, we were gone.

When I woke up in my body, the sun was about to rise. I sat there for a minute, thinking about how I was going to tell the others. "The others!" I said, jumping to my feet and started running. *But where do I go?* I thought. *Home.*

Once I reached home, I burst through the front door and ran up the stairs. I ran into the twin's bedroom, but before I could say anything, Star appeared in front of me and slapped me hard (and I mean *hard* – it hurt more than when the twins and I fought) across the face.

"Nice to see you too, Star," I said with a smile. OK, I know I probably shouldn't have smiled, as Star looked furious, but she looked so cute with it.

"Nice to see you. NICE TO SEE YOU, IS THAT ALL YOU HAVE TO SAY?! You put Sean in the hospital. He's in a coma. I only had time to help Karl; and now you waltz in here like nothing happened. I *hate* you Felix Moon! How could you do that to me and your friends?"

The smile fell off my face when she said she hated me. It was like a blow to the chest. "Please, don't say that Star," I whispered.

"Well then, you need to get your butt over to St. Christians hospital and help your best friend," Star said, cupping her hands around my sad face to make me feel better.

"I know how to save Freddy."

"HOW?" Star asked, a little louder than needed.

"I'll tell everyone once I've sorted Sean out."

Then, in the blink of an eye, we were standing next to Sean's hospital bed. Star had teleported us there.

He had tubes coming out from everywhere and a huge bandage wrapped around his head. The very bottom of his forehead peeked out from behind the dressing. The exposed skin there was a little yellow, from the bruising.

"Star I'm...I'm so sorry for what I've done. It's unforgivable, but my emotions just got the better of me and I lashed out without thinking," I said, looking down at my best friend in the state I put him in because of my moment of stupidity.

"Just heal Sean and then we can talk about forgiveness," she said flatly.

So, I put my left hand over his chest and my right hand gently on his head. I looked over at Star then closed my eyes. I opened the taps and let the energy flow through me and into Sean.

Sean wasn't completely healed, but he would be off the ventilator in a few hours, so Star took me back to my room.

The twins were there; waiting for me. The last thing they'd heard before Star took me to Sean was that I could save Freddy.

"What the hell is going on around here?" Red shouted.

Star started to fill them in on Sean when I said, "Star, I feel light-headed," and I collapsed.

When I woke up, it was dark outside, and I could feel that someone was in the bed with me. "I hope that's you Star and not one of the Satan twins," I said.

"Shush, she's not long gone to sleep," someone whispered in the dark.

I lifted my head up, but I couldn't see anyone. "Who's that?"

"Well, I'll narrow it down for you, shall I?! I'm not the one in the coma."

"Karl? Is that you?" Now that my eyes have adjusted to the darkness, I could just about make out an outline of someone sitting at the computer table.

"Yeah it's me, Felix," said Karl, leaning forward so I could see him better.

"Karl, I'm so sorry for what happened."

"What did happen, Felix? What went through your head? Using your powers on us...we couldn't defend ourselves."

Wow, Karl is really angry; and he has every right to be, I thought.

"I wasn't thinking Karl," I said feebly.

"Well I know that you dim wit...never do anything like that again, Felix."

"Oh Karl, I would never. I've got a better hold on my powers now, I promise. I went to see my Granddad Felix after...after it happened. He showed me how to detach my powers from my emotions, just to be on the safe side," I said, getting up off the bed slowly, so as not to wake Star. I walked to the door, with Karl not far behind.

I was starving. It felt like weeks since I'd last eaten something. "So, how long was I gone this time?" I said, making Karl and I a sandwich.

"Well, it's Thursday," – he paused to look up at the clock, which said 3:49 am. – "Friday even. Sean's been in a coma nearly a week."

"Crap, I really messed up this time, didn't I?"

Karl just nodded so I didn't feel bad, but I did.

We sat there eating, talking about my time in Alicade and how I had detached my powers from my emotions. I explained to Karl that if I got angry now, I couldn't use my powers until I'd reconnected them. I know it sounds silly, me talking about detaching and connecting powers, but if it keeps my friends safe then I will do it.

It was just after 10 am when Red and Ben came downstairs.

"Wow bro, the hair, we defiantly approve" Red laughed as did Ben.

I just ignored them as I knew that they wouldn't be laughing in a few minuets

"So, now that everyone apart from Sean is here, I will tell you my plan for saving Freddy. Just to let you know, no one will like it. I didn't when I heard how to do it, but it's quick and 95% pain-free for Freddy," I told them all.

"What do you mean by '95% pain-free'?" said Ben.

"Well, the way I wanted to do it was to push all my energy power to Freddy while Star exorcises whoever it is that's possessing him. But how Karl put it the other day was that, if I give him the energy, I will get kicked back and it's more than likely Freddy will die painfully. But if Freddy was close to death already, then it would be easier for Star to separate the energies, as Freddy's energy will be much weaker. Then, once Star has finished, I'll heal him."

There was silence in the kitchen.

Ben broke the silence saying, "So, you're telling me...us, that we have to *kill* our 5-year-old brother?"

"No, not kill him, bring him close to death," I clarified.

"Oh right, that sounds *so* much better. FELIX, ARE YOU FLIPPING MAD?!" Ben shouted.

"What else can we do, Ben?" I asked. "There's nothing. We don't even know who's possessing him. It could just be a small-time avatar, or it could be Kayos again."

"I think Felix has a point. It's crazy, I know, but it will work. I'll have to talk to my Dad about getting the right spell we'll need," said Star, getting up from the table.

"What do you mean by 'we'?" I said, a little confused.

"Felix, I will need help on this one," Star replied calmly. "I can't do it alone and my Dad is a very powerful wizard. He can help us."

"But he doesn't know that I'm back from the dead, does he?"

"Well, he will now," Star said; then she vanished.

"Great, all I need is Mr. Redfield getting involved," I said, putting my hands over my face.

"But if it helps Freddy then we need all the help we can get," said Red.

"I know, I know, but the fewer people that know the better"

"What about Mum and Dad? Are you going to tell them?"

"Red, are you mad?" I asked.

"You want to kill...sorry, *mostly kill*, our little brother and you're asking if I'm mad," Red said, getting a little angry.

"Sorry, but do you want to tell them the plan? " Red and Ben just shook their heads. "OK, so I will ring Dad and tell him...well, I don't really know what to say."

"Tell him that you will watch Freddy and your parents can go for a meal or something; and when they come back it should be all over," said Karl.

That sounds good, I thought; and said, "Only one little snag. Freddy, and whoever is possessing him, don't know I'm back from the dead most likely. But if Ben or Red look after him till he's asleep then I can do what needs doing," I said, still unsure and worried about what's going to happen. I keep the worry off my face, so as not to worry anyone else.

"Well, this all sounds good and all, but you need to ring Mum. She rang home every day while you were gone and she's in full-on panic mode," said Red, getting up with Ben, mirroring his every move.

"Then I'd better do it as soon as possible," I said.

"OK, well I'm going to go home for a nap, then I'm going to see Sean," said Karl.

"I'll get Star to take me to see him tonight," I said." He should be off the ventilator by now; and when I go back, I will bring him out of his coma."

"Good, because I really don't like seeing him like that," Karl said...I was too ashamed to say anything back to him.

As soon as Karl had left, I rang my parents. When my Mum picked up, she was hysterical, crying and angry all at the same time. She was mad about what I had done and told me if I ever felt myself going to that dark place again, I would have to tell someone, to which I agreed.

I told her what Karl had suggested: that they go for a meal and it should be all over once they got back. I didn't tell her what we were going to do when they were gone, even though she pushed and pushed. I told her to stay where she was until we were ready.

Two hours later, I finally got off the phone and went up to my room. I felt drained and thought a nap was called for.

When I woke up it was dark outside, so I rolled off my bed with a bump. My legs didn't feel like they had woken up yet, so I sat there, leaning my head on my bed groaning.

"Good evening to you too," Star said, making me jump.

"What the hell, Star? My heart is going a mile a minute," I said, with my hand over my chest.

She rolled her eyes. "Stop being such a drama queen, it's time to see Sean."

In three strides Star walked over to me and touched the top of my head, and we were gone.

CHAPTER SEVEN

By the morning, Sean was all healed. All he needed to do was wake up, so we waited. Whenever someone came into the room, Star would make us all invisible.

It was gone 2 pm the next day when Sean finally woke up. Let's just say he wasn't very happy to see me, and a few choice and colourful words come out of his mouth when he did. I stood there and took it because it was my fault and it's what I deserved.

Once he had calmed down enough, Star told him about the Freddy situation. Sean went crazy again, but it's only natural; everyone else had, so why would Sean be any different?

Sean got out of bed and got dressed in the clothes Star had teleported back with. "So, where are we going first?" he said.

"You're not going anywhere. You're meant to be in a coma," I said.

Sean walked over to the emergency alarm and pushed it. "You had better disappear quickly...there's going to be a lot of people in here soon."

Star touched my arm and for a second, I thought that nothing had happened. But the expression on Sean's face told me that he couldn't see us. Star had made us invisible again.

Within seconds of us disappearing, two doctors and three nurses rushed into the room and they were surprised to see Sean standing there with his arms crossed. "I'm just letting you know I'm awake and now I'm leaving," Sean said, walking past all the stunned hospital staff.

Star teleported us outside. She grabbed Sean and got us all back to my house and into my room.

"When is this all going to happen?" said Sean, sitting on the computer table's chair. I bet being in a coma still makes you tired and stiff. That's how I felt when I came back from Alicade.

"Well, we are just waiting for Star and her Father to find the spell that will exorcise whoever is possessing Freddy," I explained.

"Mr. Redfield is helping?" asked Sean, looking at me sympathetically.

"We should have it ready for next week, it's a long process," said Star.

"OK, so while you're working on Freddy, I'll call Chadwick over and work on getting his foresight back," I said. "I keep getting side-tracked. First, there was my quest to defeat Annadora, now I'm trying to get Chadwick's powers back. All while trying to find Baltazar, getting stuck in Alicade, then Freddy; and then me hurting you and Karl. So now you're OK, Star is working on Freddy. Annadora and locating Baltazar can wait while I work on Chadwick. I can focus on one thing at a time now." I breathed out heavily.

"Thank you, Felix. Chadwick wasn't very happy when you died and couldn't help him," Star said, wrapping her arms around me and kissing me on the cheek.

"It's the least I can do," I said; then she was gone.

"I'm going to rest a bit if that's OK?" Sean said.

"Yes, that's fine Sean, go right ahead."

I don't think Sean's head had hit the pillow before he was fast asleep.

Star and Chadwick turned up ten minutes later and he looked just as mad at me as he did the very first time, I had worked on him.

"Chadwick," I said curtly.

"Felix. Not going to disappear halfway through, again are you? Getting my hopes up and then stamping on them," he replied waspishly.

"In my defence, Kayos broke the portal, so I couldn't come back."

"And what have you done to your hair? you look like an idiot"

what? That's not very nice I thought to myself.

"I like it and so dose Star, that's all I really care about"

I could see Chadwick was still mad at me, but I could see in his eyes that he wasn't as mad as he previously was. "Let's just get this done," he said, sitting on my floor.

As before, I sat in front of him and he took my hand and clasped my other hand around his. Being a full avatar now, I found the spark straight away and went to work.

A few hours passed and Chadwick could feel the foreseer's energy course through him. I could tell he was excited, as his hand was shaking beneath mine. "Just a few more minutes then you should be done," I said, with a smile on my face.

"Well, stop talking and get on with it, nerd," Chadwick said, with a laugh at the end.

"All done," I said, opening my eyes and moving my hand off his. Chadwick just sat there, staring at me with a look of fear and joy.

"Chadwick, you OK?"

He shook his head. "Erm, yeah, I'm fine. It's just getting used to the feeling of having powers again. It's weird, you know!"

"Yeah, I kind of do. I know what it's like to have the avatar energy. It's like having ten cups of coffee."

"Something like that," he said. "Do you think I could use the power now, or do I have to wait to let it sink in or something?"

I laughed. "No, you can use the power now, but I only ask if you do it here so I can keep an eye on you. Just for the first time, just to make sure there's no complications."

"OK, I just need to be alone to do it. I need silence, just like you, so I can concentrate better," Chadwick said, getting up off the floor and holding his hand out for me. I took it with no hesitation.

"You can use Freddy's room or my parent's. Their room should be better for you, as there are no toys in there to distract you." I said, smiling.

"Are you saying that I've got a simple mind, that I'll get distracted by some stupid kids' toys?" Chadwick said, so serious.

"Err, well, err no, it's…"

Then Chadwick burst out laughing. "The look on your face was priceless. Where is your parent's room?"

"The door at the end of the hall," I said, shaking my head.

I noticed Sean, still fast asleep on my bed snoring quietly. I went over to my computer table and rummaged through my draws, looking for my phone. I found the charger, but no phone. I can't even remember the last time I had it. I left my room and headed to the twin's room, but I thought I would check on Chadwick first; so, I stood at my parent's bedroom door and felt for his energy. I could tell he was fine, so I knocked on the twin's door. It opened wide.

"What?" Ben said.

"Do you guys know where my phone is?"

Ben left the door open and walked over to his bedside table. He took my phone and keys out. "You left them at the last possession," he said, handing them to me.

"Thanks," I said. "It needs charging. We did keep it charged for a while, just in case you rang."

"But I was dead." "Whatever, freak," Ben said, before he slammed the door in my face.

I got back to my room and plugged the phone in. It turned straight on. 'How do I work this thing,' I thought, looking at the phone in my hands.

Once I figured it out, I sent Karl a text, saying:

Me: Hey Karl, it's Felix. I just wanted to let you know that Sean it at my house, sleeping. Chadwick's foreseeing powers have been fixed. Can you come over so we all can talk about the next step?

A minute passed, then the phone vibrated in my hands.

Karl's reply read:

> *Karl: It's strange seeing your name come up on my phone. Good to hear about Sean. I will be over shortly.*

I left the phone to charge and went to quickly check on Chadwick again; he was still fine. I walked downstairs to the kitchen and made myself a drink, filling a bottle with water to put on the bedside table for Sean.

There was a knock at the door. It was Karl. He let himself in, when I turned around, I noticed Star in the kitchen.

"When did you get here?" I said, confused. I was pretty sure she wasn't there five minutes ago.

"Just now, spell around the house remember. So, how's Chadwick?" Star asked sitting at the table.

"He's all fixed. He's in my parent's room getting reacquainted with his powers."

Star put her hand up to her mouth and started crying.

"Why are you crying, Star?" Karl asked, concerned.

"I'm just so happy Karl! Thank you so much Felix, it means so much to me. I'm in your debt."

"We can call it even; one brother for another. How's the spell going?" I queried, sitting across from her, with Karl sitting to my right.

"Well, my Father got in contact with an old friend for some advice," she began.

"Can we trust this 'friend'?" said Karl, jumping in.

"Well, he said, 'he would trust Riker with his life', so I would say we can."

"I don't know about this," I said. "There seems to be a lot of people getting involved. Me, you, Sean, Karl, the Satan twins, my parents, your brother, your Dad and now this Riker."

"What do you want, Felix? We all need help with these things. You can't exactly go on Google for this kind of stuff," Star said, getting a little annoyed.

"I know, I know. It's just this thing is getting bigger and bigger. OK, now we need to talk about something serious. How are we going to kill, stroke not kill, my little brother?" I said, shocking everyone into silence.

"What about a spell?" said Sean from behind us, making me jump.

"I think Star and her Father have enough on their plates without adding more. There's got to be something else we can try?" I said, as Sean sat down next to Star.

Karl grabbed my phone off the table and frantically started typing. *What is he doing?* I thought; then he said, "Tetrodotoxin."

"Tetro what?" I said, voicing what we were all thinking.

"Dotoxin tetrodotoxin. It's a poison from the puffer fish. It slows the heartbeat down so much that it mimics death," Karl replied.

We were all shocked. "Karl, how do you know about that?" Sean asked, looking as confused as the rest of us.

"Well, I saw it in a film."

"What films are you watching? And where are we going to get this tetrodotoxin stuff from?" replied Sean.

Karl just shrugged his shoulders; he didn't have an answer.

After we all ate, I went upstairs to check on Chadwick. I could sense that his energy had changed ever so slightly, so I opened the door as quietly as I could and peeked in.

Chadwick was standing in the middle of my parent's room, his head tilted back, looking at the ceiling, a bit like Star used to do when she was gathering energy from the setting sun. "Chadwick," I whispered. "Chadwick, are you OK?"

He was breathing heavily. I was getting a bad feeling. Something wasn't right. "Chadwick," I said, touching his arm.

"Ahhhh," he shouted.

"Felix, never pull him out of a vision too soon, he could get stuck there," Star said, pulling me away from Chadwick, who was still standing there. Now, he had his hands over his face.

"Sorry it's just... his energy feels different," I said.

"It would," Star responded. "He's not fully here. When you go into a vision, your mind goes with you. It's the same as when you go to Alicade. Your body is still here, but you're not."

"But I'm dead when I go there," I said as if it was obvious.

"I know that, you *idiot*. I'm just saying its similar. Come on, let's just leave him, he will come to us when he is ready," Star said.

I wasn't happy leaving him, but I left with Star and went to my room. Sean and Karl were already in there. We played video games for the rest of the evening, like four kids with not a care in the world.

Star took Karl home just after 10 pm and Sean not long after that.

Then she came back to my room and we lay on the bed talking

and kissing until she fell asleep.

The morning was just on the horizon when I woke up, Star still in

my arms. That's when Chadwick burst through the door.

"Felix! What's going on here?" said Chadwick angrily.

"Look Chadwick, it's not what you think. Well, actually it is, but

nothing happened; we just talked," I said, carefully moving my

arm from under Star's head and ushering Chadwick out my room,

so as not to wake her up.

"Are you going out with my sister?"

"It's a little bit more complicated than that. Let's go downstairs

and I will try to explain," I said, closing the door.

We went into the living room and sat down.

"Explain," he barked.

"When I went to Alicade with the earth element, I was told that

she was 'the one'. The one I would spend the rest of my life with."

Chadwick was silent, so I went on. "At first, I was told to stay as

far away from her – and your whole family – as a could, but I

couldn't...not from her. The first day I saw her at school I felt

drawn to her, to protect her. When I saw you both in the

cafeteria on your first day, you were having an argument –"

"She wanted to leave. She said something didn't feel right and I

told her to shut up about it," Chadwick butted in.

"Well, I wanted to protect her from you."

"Does Star know any of this?" Chadwick finally asked.

"No, she doesn't. How do I tell her something like that?" I put on an exaggerated voice. *"OH, hey Star. Just to let you know, I'm your protector and we are going to be together forever.* I've got a feeling that it won't go down very well, don't you? What if she rejects me? then what will I do?"

My breathing was short, like I couldn't breathe at all; and my heart was racing. It felt like it wanted to burst out of my chest. I started trembling and fell to my knees.

Chadwick went running off and came back with a brown bag.

"Felix, you are having a panic attack. Now listen to me. Breathe into this bag for three breaths, then breathe without the bag for five breaths."

So, I did as I was told. It took at least six attempts with the bag to slow my heart rate down enough to breathe on my own.

"Felix, do you feel better? Do you think you could stand?" Chadwick asked, being surprisingly gentle.

I just nodded. Chadwick held his hand out to help me up. "Please don't tell anyone what just happened," I said with a croaky voice.

"I won't, but what the hell, Felix? You are an avatar. I'm sure they don't get panic attacks?"

"I'm still human, aren't I?"

"What triggered it off? Was it thinking of rejection from Star?"

"I think it was," I replied. "The only other time I remember feeling like that was when I was being buried, but if I think of Star's rejection now, I don't feel panicked like before."

"That's strange. What do you think it could be?" Chadwick asked, sitting on the sofa.

I just shrugged my shoulders. "We need to change the subject. How did it go upstairs?"

"It's a long story."

Chadwick didn't tell me then, as he wanted us all together when he told us. Star walked down the stairs, rubbing her eyes. "What are you boys talking about?" she yawned.

Chadwick told her that he wanted all of us together to tell us. Star sent a quick text to Sean and Karl about coming over to talk about the vision. Sean had texted her back straight away.

"Hang on a sec," she said; then she disappeared and reappeared with Sean.

"Hey Sean," I said, surprised.

Karl couldn't meet until later that evening. I was fine with that because I wanted to go to Alicade and talk Granddad Felix. I wanted to see if he could help me with the tetrodotoxin stuff. Before I went, I rang my parents to let them know I was going there on Freddy business, which they were fine with.

I lay on my bed, Star and Sean stood each side of me. "OK, I will see you in a few minutes," I said, trying to lighten the moment, but Star still had tears in her eyes.

I closed my eyes and I concentrated on my breathing, slowing it down and visualising the white room (oh how I *love* that room). My head started spinning, so I knew it wouldn't be long before I was in the white room.

CHAPTER EIGHT

When I got to the white room I was immediately engulfed in a bright light.

"Why do you come through the visitor's entrance?" said a familiar voice from behind me.

"Kava, my brother in arms, how are you my old friend?" I asked, smiling.

"I'm very well young Felix...and yourself? Dead I see and with black hair, I like it," he chuckled ruffling my hair," he chuckled.

"Ha-ha, just for now. I need to speak to my Granddad. Do you know where he is?" I said, looking around to get my bearings.

"Are we in Falkor?" I asked.

"We are and Felix senior is at the Glacier," said Kava.

"Is everything alright?" I asked, a bit worried. The last time I was at the Glacier, Kayos broke the portal.

"Everything is fine, young Felix. He's just gone up there with a few others to collect some items for King Brogue."

"Is the King here?"

"Of course. Would you like me to take you to him?"

"Please."

We walked into the hall, where King Brogue was sitting on his throne reading. Jani was standing next to him, still looking as creepy as ever.

"Felix Jr," the King boomed. "How can I help you, my boy and with a new look, I like it"

"Thanks King Brogue"?"

So, I told him about Freddy and what we are going to do for him.

"Jani."

"Yes, my King?"

"Summon Min Lu to Falkor."

"Of course, my King," then Jani scuttled of past myself and kava.

"When I first saw you there Felix, I had a brief thought that you wanted to take me up on my offer to be the head of the Guard," said King Brogue, getting up off his overgrown throne and folding his arms around his book.

"I think I'm needed more out there at the moment," I said.

Just then the doors swung open and Mr. Creepy – Jani – and a man I've never seen before strode in.

"Thank you, Jani. That will be all. Min Lu," King Brogue said, gesturing to the man who had entered the hall with Jani. "This is Felix Jr, our Felix's great Grandson."

"It's an honour, Master Felix," said Min Lu, bowing his head.

"Min Lu, Felix Jr needs your help. He's in the market to buy some..."

Then King Brogue pointed at me, so I assumed he wanted me to finish his sentence. "Tetrodotoxin, your Majesty," I supplied.

"Your wish is my command," replied Min Lu. "It might take me a few days, though."

"Alicade days, or real-world days?" I said.

"I am deceased in the real world," said Min Lu, a little confused.

"Felix, when a person naturally dies in the real world, they cannot go back," said Kava.

"So that's why my body was perfectly preserved when I went back to it after being stuck here all those years," I said, finally understanding.

"Precisely."

"I'll come back in a few hours then," I made to leave.

"Felix wait, why not stay here? We can catch up. I know Kava hasn't seen you in a long time; and we have those little flavoured puffs you loved," said King Brogue.

So, I stayed. It would only be a few hours in the real world; and everyone knows I'm here. We caught up and I told them all about my situation with Freddy and about the bond with Star, but I neglected to tell them about Chadwick – me giving him his foresight back.

I'd been in Alicade all day and now the night drew closer. I was getting tired, what with all the larking about with Kava and King

Brogue. I could see, in the corner of the room, Jani looking as creepy as ever.

"So Brogie, where can I crash?" I asked, knowing full well that Jani would be fuming in his corner. He hates it when people (mainly me) do not address the King by his 'rightful name', as he calls it.

"Your room is still as you left it, young Felix," the King replied.

"OK cool. I'm going to go up now, I'm shattered."

I said my goodbyes to King Brogue and gave my one fingered goodbye to Jani. Kava walked me to my old room. "Goodnight Felix. It's nice to have you back, even though it's only for a little while," he said.

"It's nice to be back, it's so much calmer here. Out there it feels like one thing after another, but here it's like a little holiday."

"Well, I hope you don't leave it too long next time between visits."

"Why don't you come visit me in the real world? My friends, they would love to finally meet you. I feel like I talk about you all the time." Kava frowned and looked down to the floor. "What's up Kava? Is it something I said?" I asked, trying to think back to what I'd just said to him.

"Felix, I'm dead in the real world. I cannot go through the portal," he responded sadly.

"There has to be away?"

"If there was, don't you think we would know?"

"I suppose," I said quietly. I didn't know what else to say.

"Goodnight Felix."

"Night, Kava."

I walked into my old room. It was eerie. Everything was still in the exact same place as I left it. The only difference was that there was a thin layer of dust everywhere.

My suit of armour was still stood in the corner, but it wasn't dusty like everything else. It looked like it had been polished regularly, shiny and gold. It looked like new, some of the little old battle scars had been knocked out or sewed up; but the big sword hole was still in the right-hand side, where one of Kayos' men had got me when I was helping someone else in trouble. I lifted my top up to see the scar that I had gotten them, but it wasn't there. *Where's that gone?* I thought, but then I caught a glimpse of myself in the mirror. I was 16 again, because I'd returned to the real world. I'd been stabbed when I was last in Alicade and I'd been 20 then. All the time I'd spent here felt more like a dream than reality the only thing that's changed was my hair colour.

I got in my old bed. I had forgotten how much I hate this bed, it's so uncomfortable.

It only felt like I'd closed my eyes for a split second before the horns were going off in the morning.

"No, no, no, NO!" I said, putting the covers over my head.

After an hour of refusing to get out of bed, I could smell bacon being fried. It wafted under my door so, with my eyes still half closed, I let my nose lead the way to the dining hall.

"Morning, young Felix." said King Brogue.

He's always so cheerful at this time of the morning. I just grumbled. "It feels like I never slept a wink all night. I'm still so tired." I yawned and rubbed my eyes.

"Well, eat some breakfast then rest a little more, as I've had word from Masguard and Min Lu will have the drug you require by this evening."

"That's fantastic! Where's Masguard?" I asked. I had never heard of such a place when I was last here.

"Felix. Alicade is not the only realm; there are five altogether. There's Alicade and the Glacier, which you know of, but there's also Masguard, Camforge and a Waterfall. Alicade is the largest and it's where I have resided for the last 300 or so years. I rule the highest overall five realms," King Brogue explained.

"What do you mean you rule the highest?" I questioned him.

"All the other realms have their own royalty, but I rule over them all."

How did I not know this? I'd lived here for nearly seven years and never knew about the other realms. I vaguely remember Kava telling me he was from Camforge, but I just thought it was a place in the real world. I wasn't that good at geography at school.

"Where is Kava anyway? He never misses breakfast." I said, cramming some eggs in my mouth like I'd not eaten for a week.

"You will choke if you put any more in your mouth, Jr," said Granddad Felix, as he sat down next to me.

"Granddad," I said as I hugged him.

"Do you have the item I requested?" King Brogue said to him.

"I do, my King, here," said Granddad Felix, pulling a heavy leather-bound book from his bag; but instead of giving the book to the King, he placed it in front of me.

"What's this?" I asked curiously. Looking at the book closer, I could just make out the same mark I used to draw all the time. It's the one I'd drawn in front of Star at school when I'd first met her, before I knew anything about who I really was. Excluding the middle section, it looks like the mark that has started to appear on my back.

"Felix, it's the journal of Baltazar. I had it frozen into the Glacier so it wouldn't fall into the wrong hands. Please take great care of it," King Brogue said, standing up to leave,

"But sire, he's only a stupid kid," said Jani, walking over from the corner. What is it with this creep always lurking in the corner of the room?

"It's OK Jani, I trust he will make the right choices."

Jani shot me a dirty look.

"Why are you giving me this?" I said, a little puzzled as to why he would do such a thing.

"You're a mod avatar and I am not. It will be of more use in your hands than mine." Then King Brogue walked away, closely followed by his shadow, Jani.

I was confused. What did he mean by, 'more use in my hands'? I gently put my hand on the book and felt a shock of energy come off it. "What the hell was that?" I said, quickly moving my hand off the book.

"Felix, no one has ever looked inside the book," said Kava, who sat on the other side of me with his overflowing plate of food.

"What do you mean by 'no one'? How can no one have looked inside, it's only a book? Is it to do with the energy that comes off the book?" I said. I was a little confused.

"The book doesn't open for us, Felix. What do you mean the book's energy?" asked Granddad Felix.

I took a breath and explained, saying, "When I touched the book, I felt a zap of energy from it."

Granddad Felix put his hand on the cover. "I don't feel anything," he said, sounding puzzled.

I must of imagined it, I thought to myself, so I put my hand on the book again. There was definitely energy flowing from the book. I opened the cover. Granddad Felix gasped beside me and said, "Oh my, Felix, you've done it! what does it say?"

The handwriting was like a script. It was incredible. "Look for yourself."

I pushed the book towards him. "The pages are blank," he said, in an astonished tone.

"How can they be blank? I can see the writing."

"Then you must be the only one who can read it," said Kava, between mouthfuls of food.

It was strange being able to read something that nobody else could, I could tell them what it says.

"So, Felix, do you like junior's hair?" Kava said still shovelling food in his mouth, "I did notice it last time he popped over but he wasn't in the best state to have asked, I like it, you look just like me when I was younger" Granddad Felix said rustling my hair just like Kava did.

I excused myself from the table and took the book back up to my room. I sat on the bed with the book in front of me, in two minds whether to read it. I wanted to know what it might say about being a mod avatar, but this book was Baltazar's journal and he wasn't exactly a pillar of the community, was he?

"Come on Felix, just read the bloody thing," I said to myself as I opened the book.

It read:

This is my journal.

It tells the story of how I came to be the ruler of all men and avatars alike.

I can't remember when I first discovered I had all of these powers, but it was the best feeling ever. I refined them within the first few years of possessing them. Then, once I was 25, I stopped ageing. I looked the same at 40 as I had at 25.

Some long years passed. When I was 89, I wanted to try and see if I could create more people like me – avatars.

I was fed up with being alone.

I had used my energy power to help people when I worked in the hospitals.

It was 1763 and I was working in my third hospital. I had to move a lot because I was meant to be 36, but only looked 25 and I did not want the attention of others.

There was this one gentleman suffering from a knife wound to his belly and he was definitely going to die without my help, so I took him back to my house and went to work.

I had healed his wounds using the energy I have inside me while he was unconscious. Then I split my powers in half in my mind and pushed my powers into him. It took several attempts before it worked.

Once he had woken up, he was overwhelmed with all the new power he now had; and so, I took three of the powers back and just left him with one. I worked with him for months before he could control it.

That gentleman's name was Felix Moon.

That kicked me back to reality. That's my name and my great Grandfather's. How far back does my name go? I read on for a while longer. Baltazar went on about how he found the portal in

1897, when the house he and 'his Felix' shared was set on fire by a gang of hooligans who'd tried, unsuccessfully, to steal money from them. They both died in the fire and ended up in Alicade. Baltazar could still travel through the portal between both worlds, but Felix couldn't, so Baltazar had found a way. If he came to the real world and pulled Felix's energy through the portal with him then Felix would appear. I couldn't wait to tell Kava that I now had a way of taking him with me back to the real world.

I flicked through some random pages, not really looking at what it said, until I got to the bit about Balthazar being a King:

I am the true King of all.
No puny avatar will be King, only the mod avatar will be the one,
true King.

What did that mean? Did it mean I should be King? I just shook my head. That can't be right, should I bring it up with King Brogue or with Granddad Felix? Both ideas sounded crazy, they wouldn't believe me as they couldn't read it in the book, so I come to the conclusion that I was going to speak to Kava when we got back to the real world.

I closed the book, overwhelmed with it all. I noticed it was starting to get dark outside, so I picked up the book and went looking for King Brogue. I didn't have to look far; he was sat on his throne, talking to Jani and Min Lu.

"Jr, how's the book?" he enquired.

"Interesting, to say the least," I responded. "Have you got the tetrodotoxin? I'm getting a little bit nervous that my friends think there might be something wrong, what with me not coming back sooner."

"Of course, Master Felix," said Min Lu, handing me a little vial of clear liquid. "No more than three millilitres, Master Felix. I have diluted it down, but It's still very potent."

"Thank you, Min Lu, you are a lifesaver! I have no money to give you for it."

"Money is not needed, Master Felix. The debt has been paid in full."

I looked at King Brogue, knowing he'd paid it for me. "Thanks again, Min Lu. Your help means a lot to me." "It's my pleasure. Is there anything else you need from me my King?" he said, turning to King Brogue.

"That will be all Min Lu. Thank you very much," replied the King. Min Lu bowed his head and left.

"Thanks, Brogue, for all you have done for me. I don't know how to repay you," I said, genuinely grateful.

"Just go out there and be the best I know you can be."

"I'll try. I've only got one question. How do I take this stuff out there to the real world?" I asked, holding up the book and the vial. I'd never brought anything home from Alicade before.

"Just hold onto them tight and visualize holding them when you're out there," said King Brogue, getting up from his throne.

"OK, I'll do that. Goodbye, King Brogue. I will try to visit more often in the future."

"You'd better," said Kava from behind me.

I turned around and hugged him, whispering, "You're coming with me."

Kava looked puzzled and was about to speak, when I put my finger up to my lips and shushed him.

"Goodbye Felix. Take care of yourself and that family of ours," my Granddad said, stepping toward me.

"Will do, Granddad," I said, hugging him tightly.

I sat on the floor with the book on my lap and the vile in my hand and visualized my room, with my comfy bed – oh how I've missed it being here. It's strange. It's the little things you miss the most when you're away, but I made sure the book and vile were at the forefront of my mind. It didn't take long for the room to start spinning and for me to get lightheaded. With my last breath in Alicade, I took my first in the real world, still with the vial in one hand and the book on my chest.

I had done it!

CHAPTER NINE

I woke up and there was no one in the room with me, which I thought was a little bit strange. I got up off my bed and headed downstairs.

I found them all in the living room watching a film. I stood there for 10 minutes before Karl looked over at me.

"Look, Felix is back," he said, getting up.

"I've come bearing gifts," I said, holding out the book and vial. When I told them about the book, Sean tried to open it. Of course, he couldn't. Then everyone else tried and failed. I continued, "I've got to go do something before we get down to the business of saving Freddy; and before I tell you more about the book."

I told them to stay downstairs while I went back to my room.

What did the book say? 'Pull his energy through the portal', I thought.

"How hard can that be?" I said to myself, closing my eyes.

I knew what Kava's energy felt like, I had healed him enough times when we were fighting at the portal. I felt his energy in my head, like a soft hum. I let it fill me and then it was gone. I slowly

opened my eyes and there he was, stood right there in front of
me.

I jumped off my bed. "Oh my god, I can't believe it worked!" I
exclaimed.

"Felix, where am I?" Kava asked uncertainly.

"I told you I would find a way," I said in reply.

"Am I in the real world?" said Kava, still a little confused.

"Yes, yes you are my friend. Baltazar's journal, it told me how to
do it"

"I'd forgotten the feeling of going through the portal. it's not very
nice is it?" Kava joked.

"Come on. Let me introduce you to my other friends."

I walked back into the living room, with Kava close behind me.

"Everyone, I would like you to meet Kava, he's from Alicade,"

After all the introductions, I filled Kava in on what's been going on

with Freddy. "OK, now that we are all here, I want to tell you all

what I saw," Chadwick said. "Erm, Kava, don't freak out, but

Chadwick and Star are Annadora's children. Star is a witch and

Chadwick has now his foresight back."

Kava stood up, shaking his head. "How can you be in cahoots with
them?"

"But they are *with* me on this quest. They want to help me stop
her."

"But not kill her," Chadwick interrupted.

"What do you mean?" I asked.

"You told us that you have to kill Annadora," Chadwick said.

"That's what Aires told me, that it's been foreseen that I kill her. Was he lying?"

Chadwick nodded. "He must have been, because she ends up getting held in a place called Falkor. I saw it in my first vision, just after you gave me my foresight back."

Kava and I just looked at each other.

"Felix, do you know where that is?" asked Karl, making me look away from Kava.

"Erm yeah, it's in Alicade, where King Brogue lives."

Chadwick caught my eye. He was shaking his head slightly. I think I knew what he was going to say next. He was going to talk about how I was supposed to be King, as apparently, it's my right, being a mod avatar. He'd obviously seen that too. I just stared at him, hoping he wouldn't let that little bit of information out.

"When and where does it all go down?" said Star.

"In the next few weeks," replied Chadwick. "It looks like it happens in Drake Forest."

"God why is it always in Drake Forest?" asked Karl, slumping back in his chair.

"That's not all," Chadwick continued slowly, choosing his next words carefully. "Not all of us will come out of this alive."

I closed my eyes so no one could see the pain in them. "Who doesn't make it?" There was no answer, so I opened my eyes.

"Chadwick, who is it?" I said, through gritted teeth.

Chadwick's eyes flicked over at Karl. "No, no, NO! IT'S NOT GOING TO HAPPEN, NO ONE IS GOING TO DIE!" I didn't mean for it to come out all shouty and angry, but I wanted what I'd said to be true so badly.

"Felix, if it's been foreseen then…" Star began.

"No Star. I'm not going to let it happen. I read somewhere that a vision is not a fixed point in time."

"That's right, but it's very hard to change."

"I get that, but in your vision, was Kava with us?"

Chadwick looked up at the ceiling then looked straight at me.

"No. I've seen this play out many times and Kava was not there."

"It's because I have Baltazar's journal," I said excitedly.

"Everything is about to change."

I was *not* going to let one of my best friends die without a fight!

I took Chadwick to the kitchen so I could talk to him in private.

"Chadwick, did you see me as the King of Alicade in your vision?" I asked, not really wanting to know the answer.

"I did, Felix. What's going on?" I told him what the journal said about me being the rightful King because I'm a mod avatar. "Have you told anyone else?"

"No, I was going to talk to Kava about it."

"But if you're the rightful King, you should take it, it's your right."

"I don't know if I want it, Chadwick. It turned Baltazar crazy with power. I don't want that to happen to me."

"But it won't, we're all with you and we *won't* let that happen," said Chadwick, putting his hand on my shoulder. He was being a great deal friendlier towards me since our conversation about Star being my soulmate.

"It's not that easy. It would mean staying there – in Alicade. I would have to leave everyone here. We don't have time to think about that right now. Tell me how Karl dies?"

"Well…erm, Annadora drowns him. Control over water is the only power she possesses."

"So, what if I give him the wind power? Then he could breathe underwater, do you think that would work?"

"Does he think what would work?" asked Karl, interrupting us. I couldn't look at him knowing we were talking about his future, his death.

"Felix and I are brainstorming something, go back into the living room," said Chadwick.

"OK, I'm just getting some drinks," Karl said, looking at me strangely. I still couldn't look at him. "Felix, are you OK?"

"I'm fine, Karl."

Karl grabbed a six-pack of Coca-Cola then walked out of the kitchen.

"I can't let him die, Chadwick. I've put them all through so much lately, I just can't."

"We *will* figure this out. OK, I'm going back upstairs to see if the vision has changed, what with Kava being here."

With that, Chadwick left me standing in the kitchen alone. I stayed there a little longer, just so I could compose myself. Walking back into the living room, I could tell that Kava had fitted in nicely with my other friends. They were all joking around.

"Hey Felix, did you know Kava has never tried a Coca-Cola before?"

"Has he not?" I asked, knowing full well that they didn't have Coca-Cola in Alicade.

"And while you two girls were gossiping in the kitchen, my Dad rang. He said the spell is ready, so I told him we will be ready for tomorrow," said Star.

"Wow, that's great news," I said in the most enthusiastic voice I could muster.

Later that night, Star took Sean and Karl home, Kava had already passed out on the sofa hours ago and Chadwick was still upstairs.

"So, are you going to tell me what's going with you?" Star said, hugging me from behind.

I held her hand and pulled her in front of me. "I love you, you know, that right?"

"I know, I love you too, what's up, Felix? You're acting strange."

"It's Karl, he's the one that doesn't make it."

Star was stunned into silence. Tears started rolling down her cheeks.

"Hey, hey, hey, it's going to be OK. Chadwick and I are working on something, don't cry," I said, trying to soothe her. I leant forward and gently, I kissed her.

We were making out when Chadwick walked into the living room.

"Well, I've looked...erm Felix, I hope you're not kissing my sister?" Star quickly moved away from me. "Who I kiss is none of your business," I said, with a smile. I knew Chadwick was only joking, as he knew what the situation was between me and Star now.

"Well, anyway, sorry I have to say this, but he still dies." I look up at the ceiling, trying not to let my emotions get the better of me.

"Even with Kava here, it still happens. I'm so sorry Felix," Chadwick continued.

"He's not going to die...does he still drown?"

"Yes," Chadwick said, with a strange look in his face.

"I will give him the power to possess the wind then, when she drowns him, he can blow her out the way; or even make a wind orb and he can breathe through it under the water." I said. My mind's racing with all these different ideas about how to save Karl.

"You know what, that might work," Star said, standing beside me. I had forgotten that she was there. "But the question is: how are we going to give him the wind power without alerting him to the fact that something's going to happen to him? He might work out that he's the one who's going to die."

"I will give it to everyone; and you too, if you want it. I'm a mod avatar and I can give it to whoever I want."

Star looked at me, afraid.

"It's OK Star. I'm not going to go crazy with power, but I would do anything to keep you all safe," I said.

"I won't let you go the same way as Baltazar," she said in response before we kissed.

Cough, cough. The sound came from Chadwick's direction. "I am still standing here you know."

"Sorry mate. I just can't help myself sometimes," I joked.

"Well, I'm OK with your relationship, as long as you don't keep kissing in front of me. Dad, on the other hand...I don't think he will approve."

The blood ran from my face. Mr. Redfield would kill me if he found out about Star and me, he didn't like me at the best of times.

"Chadwick, Dad does not need to know," warned Star.

I was nodding my head in agreement.

"Star, you know Dad wants to fight with us...and as soon as he sees you two together, he'll realise what's going on."

"He's not fighting, he can help with the spells and that's it, no fighting," she said vehemently.

I thought to myself that it was best to stay out of their family drama.

"I think he has a right to fight, as it *is* his wife and we all know he still loves her, even with all the crap she's done to everyone in the past. He still wants to help her in any way he can; and it's not your decision. It's Felix's decision," said Chadwick, looking straight at me.

I had zoned out and hadn't been paying much attention. I noticed that they were both staring at me. "Erm, what?" I asked.

"Can you tell *him* that my Dad can't fight with us?" Star said, pointing her finger at Chadwick.

"Can you tell *her* that it's not her fight and it's not her decision," Chadwick said.

I just stood there like an idiot.

"Well?" Star demanded, folding her arms across her chest.

Oh no, angry Star, I thought. "Erm, it's not just my fight. We are all involved, so it should go to a vote."

"Well, we will take a vote tomorrow," said Star, still angry; before she stormed out the house.

"Erm, OK, bye Star," I said, shocked.

Chadwick looked after her and said, "She's just a hot-head, she will be OK. I'm going to get some sleep and we'll try again tomorrow. Night, Felix."

"Night Chadwick," I said. Then he left too.

I left Kava asleep on the sofa because I know what the time difference feels like between Alicade and here. My bed felt like heaven, so soft and warm and cosy. I don't want to leave it for a week – that's a real-world week, not an Alicade week.

CHAPTER TEN

I woke up with Star standing at the end of my bed. It made me jump. "Oh my god, Star! What the hell? How long have you been standing there being all creepy?"

"Not long, but I need to talk to you about my Dad. He can't fight with us. If he sees you kill her, he will lose it. Would you want your Father fighting with us?" she asked.

"No. No, I wouldn't, but your Dad does have powers and mine don't. I know you want to keep him safe, but I personally think he should get involved, as he knows Annadora inside and out. I think he will distract her just long enough for me to get her, but we will still put it to a vote. Like I said last night, it's not just my fight, we're all a part of it." I could see that she was upset, but I think she understood where I was coming from.

"Anyway, who said I'm going to kill Annadora? I thought Chadwick said that she gets held at Falkor in Alicade?"

"That's right, oh god, I'm so confused about all this now. I don't know what to think."

"Come on Star, you can't flake out now, you're the only one holding me together. With all this craziness, all I have to do it think about you, or Freddy and I calm down; and I can think straight. So, let's get Freddy fixed, then we can worry about your Mother and Father after," I said, putting my arm around her.

We hugged and kissed for a while until my hunger got the best of me. Star left to talk to the others about the vote and to tell them to come to mine at 7 pm.

Red and Ben were in the kitchen, so I filled them in on the voting.

"But we won't be fighting, will we? Because we have no powers and we are rubbish at hand-to-hand combat," said Red, slumping in his chair.

"What if I told you that you could have an avatar power? Which one would you have?" I asked.

They both said in unison, "fire." How did I know they were going to say that? I did call them the Satan Twins, after all.

"Why do you want to know? Are you going to give us powers?" Ben says, all excited.

"Well, yes, but only one. Not the firepower though, as it's tricky to master. All normal avatars can only use fire when calm, but I have to be angry, so I would prefer not to give that power…Karl is going to have the wind power."

"But he didn't want the powers before. What makes you think he will want the powers now?" asked Ben.

Red must have seen the pain in my face, because he said, "Is something going to happen to him?"

I just nodded. That's all I could do, because if I spoke, I would probably cry.

"OK, so when do we get our powers?"

I coughed the thickness out my throat and replied, "Erm, we can try now. It might take some time, but we can try".

It didn't take as long as I first thought, because I now know how to split the element; and not push my whole power into the host. I gave Ben the wind power; and Red the waterpower. "OK boys, I'm only warning you once…and once *only*. Abuse this power, or show anyone; and I mean *anyone,* I will take the powers straight off you, you hear me?"

"But the people involved in this, we can show them?"

"Yes Ben, you can show them. I'm going to need your help to try to convince Karl to take a power from me, as I know he will freak when I tell him he has to have one. I can't just give it to him without him knowing."

"It's OK Felix, we will talk to him when he comes later," Red said, putting his hand on my shoulder.

It's the first time I'd seen compassion in their eyes. They really wanted to help me. It overwhelmed me and I couldn't help the tears that escaped from my eyes. "I can't let Karl die; it's my fault his involved."

"It's OK Felix, we will deal with Karl. When Freddy is fixed, we are going to Drake Forest to train."

I laughed at that notion. "I think I will come with you; you will probably kill your silly selves."

"You're probably right there, bro," Red laughed.

"Come on then, let's do this," Ben said, all excited.

So, the three of us went to Drake Forest, to the clearing. I hate this place now, but it's a good training ground. I showed the twins how to do simple tasks, like how to make a wind orb for Ben; and how to draw the water up from the ground for Red.

I rang my Mother to tell her that the twins will come and get Freddy tonight at 6.

The twins were getting good at their new abilities by the time we had to leave Drake Forest. They went to get Freddy and I went home to hide in my room, so Freddy didn't see me.

Ben put Freddy to bed when they got back with him, I told Ben and Red to put the tetrodotoxin stuff in his warm milk for bed and it wasn't long before he came in with Red to tell me that he was asleep. I texted Star that it was time and one by one Sean, Karl, Chadwick, Calvin (her Father) and Star turned up in my room. Having Calvin standing in my room was very daunting, he's just so big and scary.

"OK, now that everyone is here, it has come to my attention that Mr. Redfield wants to join the fight and I want to put it to a vote. I vote yes," I said.

We all voted yes, even Star; she must have thought about what I said about needing her Father to help us.

"OK, Mr. Redfield you're in. Now it's time for you to help my little brother," I concluded.

He nodded and said, "Where is the boy?"

"He's in his room, I will show you," said Ben.

"Are you ready, Star?" Calvin asked.

"I'll be there in just a second," she said.

Calvin nodded his head and followed Ben.

Star turned to me and said, "Are you ready for this, Felix? Try not to think that it's Freddy. It might make it better for you, emotionally."

"OK, I'll try."

Star put her arms around my waist. "We will save Freddy," she said, then kissed me gently on the lips.

We heard Calvin call for Star to hurry up.

"OK, stay here and I will call you when it's time for you to come in. I love you," Star told me.

"I love you too," I said, as my voice broke and the tears streamed down my face.

Star wiped my tears away and gave me a quick kiss. Then she was gone.

I stood there for a few minutes trying to compose myself, when Ben walked back into the room. "How was it in there?" I asked.

"They've laid Freddy on the floor with candles all around him. Mr. Redfield started chanting in a different language that I didn't recognise. I needed to get out of there I didn't like seeing Freddy like that, I don't envy your powers Felix, or the weight that must be on your shoulders," he said. He put his hand on my shoulder. "Thanks, Ben. Please don't forget what you said about helping me with that matter about powers."

I quickly glanced at Karl, who was spinning on my computer chair. "Consider it done," said Ben.

I slowly walked towards Freddy's room. As I got to his door, it opened. It was Star who came out. "Oh god, Felix, you scared me. I was just about to come and get you, we are ready for you," she said.

I poked my head in the door and, just as Ben said, Freddy was laying on the floor with candles around him. His head was on his dinosaur pillow and he had his favourite light brown teddy bear under his left arm. I knew it would have been Star that made Freddy more comfortable.

I stepped in the room and tried to feel for Freddy's energy. It was weak, really weak. I could hardly feel it, so the tetrodotoxin stuff must be working.

"Come on Felix, my Dad has got everything ready. We just need to say the incantation, but I do have to warn you, it's not going to be pleasant to watch," said Star, taking my hand and giving it a little squeeze.

"I can do it, I need to do it, for Freddy."

Star nodded her head and took me over to Freddy. I sat at the top and put my hand on Freddy's forehead. He was sweating, but cold at the same time.

"OK Felix, I know this is going to be hard for you, but Star and I know what we are doing. When I tell you to, push as much energy into him as you can," said Calvin.

I just nodded.

"Please move back a bit Felix," he said.

I did as I was told.

"Benedicam Freddy simul undique," they began to chant. With those words, Freddy started to lift up off the floor, till he was at least 3ft off the ground. Star must have seen the panic across my face. "Felix, turn around, don't watch this," she said gently.

I turned halfway through her sentence; I didn't want to see Freddy in distress. I didn't know if he was in pain or if the tetrodotoxin stuff would numb him. They spoke some more strange words. Calvin went first, with Star repeating every word. Freddy started screaming, but the voice coming from him was too female to be his.

"Annadora, leave this child!" Calvin shouted.

"I'm disappointed in you Calvin. We were so good together, such a waste." It was Freddy's voice, but not his words; another scream from Freddy.

"Anna, he is a baby, just leave him."

Star chimed in, saying, "Mum, leave him, or I will do something drastic."

"Ha, ha, ha, ha! What is little Star going to do to me?"

There was more hysterical laughter.

"Cor sistenda, NUNC!" Star screamed.

"STAR NO! FELIX NOW, DO IT NOW!" Calvin shouted.

When I turned around, Star was falling to the floor and Calvin had Freddy in his arms. I put my hands over Freddy's heart. It had stopped beating, but I couldn't think about that now, so I pushed so much energy into him that I got dizzy. Then there it was, the best feeling in the world, a little flutter of Freddy's heart. Tears streaming down my face, I cried, "Come on Freddy, come on."

I closed my eyes and gave it one last push. Freddy took a breath and started coughing and crying.

I must have blacked out because the next thing I remember is Calvin throwing a glass of water over my face. I woke up with a start.

"What the...?" I spluttered.

"Sorry Felix, but you weren't waking up," said Calvin, by way of explanation.

"Where is Freddy?" I asked.

"He's in bed asleep, the exorcism was a success."

"Where's Star?"

"She's...OK."

I didn't like the pause, but I didn't want to push him, as Calvin still

scares me. I got up off the floor and noticed I was in

my parent's bedroom. I walked out with Calvin close behind me.

"I'm glad Freddy is OK, but I need to leave to rest," he said,

sounding exhausted. Then he was gone.

I slowly crept into Freddy's room. After what we'd put him

through, I didn't want to leave him, so I curled up next to him. I

couldn't quite fit. I had poured so much energy into him I was

drained and before I knew it, I was asleep.

In the morning, I could feel something pulling at my hair.

Opening my eyes, still blurry from sleep, I heard, "Fix, you home

now?"

"Yes, Freddy, I'm home and I'm not going anywhere," I replied.

"I missed you Fix, I Hun-gee."

"I missed you too, Mini-Me. Let's go get some breakfast".

Freddy climbed on my back as I took him downstairs and into the

kitchen. "Hey, Freddy. You feeling better?" asked Star, who was

sitting at the table with Red and Ben. It was strange looking at the

Satan twins, as they looked so different. They had none

of their Goth make up on and Red's long hair was tied back.

"Yep, yep, yep, look Fix got black hair now." Freddy laughed.
I've missed that little laugh, all the time in Alicade, all I thought about was Star and Freddy, his little laugh made me so happy.

"I can see that buddy. Do you want some breakfast?" asked Ben.

"Cheerio's and flakes."

"Cheerio's and flakes it is."

Freddy jumped down off my back and went to sit on his chair at his little blue table. The last time I saw Freddy at this table he was possessed and unhappy, but now he was bouncing, waiting for his food and playing with his little Marvel figures.

"I didn't think you were going to come over today," I asked Star, leaning down and kissing her on the lips.

"Err, Fix does kissing," said Freddy, covering his face.

"I never left last night. When I passed out, they put me in your bed," Star explained.

"What happened last night? Why did you pass out?" I asked.

"I was linked with Freddy and I stopped my heart, which stopped his."

"But why would you do that?" I asked confused.

"It was the only way, as Annadora was not letting him go. She was killing him, so I had to do something drastic."

"But what if that hadn't have saved him?" I said, getting a little angry.

"My Dad was there, so he would have done something to help. Felix, I'm sorry, but I would do it again if needs be." Star said unapologetically.

I stood there for a minute, looking over at Freddy. I leant down and kissed Stars head. "Thank you," I said. "When we were in the room, you were chanting in another language, what was it?"

"It was Latin. My Dad wants everyone together at five, so he can stop Annadora from ever doing anything like this again."

"My parents will be back by then."

"He will want to protect them too. Everyone needs protecting."

It felt like old times, like a normal morning, but different at the same time. My life has changed so drastically in the last two or so years (or about 13 Alicade years). I've become a full-fledged mod avatar; I have the girl of my dreams by my side getting me through everything; my parents know everything, but I don't think they fully understand my mission. At least they realise that whatever I do needs to be done. And my two best friends, Sean and Karl, they have been with me from the start. I've hurt them terribly and they still stand by me through thick and thin. And, last but not least, there's Kava. My friend and mentor, he's taught me so much.

My Mum and Dad got home just after 11 am and they were over the moon (bad pun) that Freddy was back to normal. I told them of Mr. Redfield's involvement and that he was coming over to put

an anti-possession spell on us all, so that what Annadora did to
Freddy can't happen to anyone else.

Mum has been in the kitchen all afternoon baking cookies, cakes,
pies. You name it, she's most probably baked it.

It was 4:50 when Mr. Redfield knocked on the door with Star and
Chadwick.

Dad answered the door and took them into the living room,
where everyone that was involved were sat: me, Sean, Karl, Kava,
Red, Ben, and Freddy. We were playing on the floor with Freddy's
cars.

"I will go and get Sue so we can get started," said Dad, leaving the
living room.

"It will take a few minutes to set up the spell. I'll let you know
when it's done," said Calvin, walking over to the far corner of the
room. He moved everything off the side table, which was next to
the black leather sofa that Sean and Kava were currently sat on.
Then he started drawing a symbol on it in chalk.

Just then, a high-pitched screech came from behind us. I don't
know about anyone else, but it scared the hell out of me. "What
on *earth* are you doing, Calvin?"

"It's OK, Mum. Mr. Redfield knows what he's doing," I said, trying
to calm her down.

Mr. Redfield turned to my Mum and said, "I just need a flat
surface, watch. Hocsymboloinnominebenedictus Hellsolo."

Star's head snapped up and she looked straight at her Father, as did Chadwick. "Dad, what are you doing?"

"It's OK, Chadwick. Like Felix said, I know what I am doing. I need to keep my family safe."

"But channelling Hellsolo?"

"I will be fine, trust me," Calvin said, putting a bronze bowl down on the table where the chalk symbol had disappeared.

"But Hellsolo is not the right way," Star said, walking towards him.

"Stop there, Star, this space is charged," Calvin warned her.

That stopped Star in her tracks. I grabbed her arm and pulled her back towards me.

Chadwick looked at Calvin with so much anger and rage in his face. I took the opportunity to whisper in Star's ear, "What is Hellsolo?"

Calvin was chanting, still, in a language, I still didn't understand. Star replied without taking her eyes of her Father. "It's not a what, it's a who; Hellsolo is the power priest he has inside of him. It makes him more powerful. When Dad casts a spell after calling on Hellsolo, the spell binds to his lifeforce. So, this protection spell; it will protect us until he dies. It can never be broken until then."

"Wow, and why is that a bad thing?"

She turned to me and said, "You know my hair changes colour with the more power I have?" I nodded. "Well, I have a Hellsolo power priest inside me too. I'm just worried it will take him over again."

"Oh right…AGAIN? What do you mean again?" I said, quieter this time.

"It was when my Mother fell off the rails. My Dad conjured Hellsolo and it consumed him. He fought so hard to control it. I was consumed too, that's why I don't like to have too much power. It's too hard to control the Hellsolo priest."

"So, you're telling me that you have someone inside of you?" She just nodded as she looked back over to where Calvin was stood, her eyes nearly bulging out of her head. I looked over as well; and he had a blade up to his left hand. I quickly turned to my Mum and said, "Don't let Freddy watch this bit." But they were already on it. Dad had already swooped down, picked Freddy up and left the living room, with my Mum close behind.

I turned back around. Calvin was slowly cutting his hand. "Protect me, protect my family and protect the Moons. Hellsolo protects all," said Calvin, slicing deeper into his right hand. The blood was starting to pool in his hand. Putting the knife down, he held his left hand about 2ft above his right. As he chanted the Latin phrase for the second time, the blood started flowing upwards towards his left hand. The blood just hovered there, not quite touching his hand. I was mesmerized by the thick red liquid as it twisted and rippled around in mid-air.

The blood had stopped flowing upwards now. As he moved his right hand away, I noticed that the wound from the knife cut was gone. He started lowering his hand towards the bronze bowl, which had all sorts of herbs and some sort grey grainy powder in it. I hadn't even seen him put that stuff in there.

The metallic smell of blood started to fill the air. The blood pool had started dripping into the bowl, slowly at first, then faster and faster. When it made contact with the ingredients in the bowl, it crackled like a sparkler and started smoking. It smelled sickly sweet. Once all the blood was in the bowl, Calvin waved his hands over it and spoke in Latin again. Note to self: *learn Latin.* The only word I knew was Hellsolo, which I know is bad.

I glanced over at Star. She was crying, so I put my arm over her shoulder and kissed her cheek. It wasn't much of a gesture, but it made her smile, even if only for a fraction of a second.

Looking back over at Calvin, I noticed that his eyes had turned bright red. It was so freaky, but I suppose it was like looking at my silver-grey eyes. I will always remember when I started school. By the end of first grade, Sean and Karl were already friends. The principal had walked me into room H3, where Mrs. Coolie was taking registration.

"Morning Mrs. Coolie. Sorry to disturb you," he'd said.

"That's OK Principal York. Class?" she'd responded.

"Good morning Principal York," the whole class had said, in perfect unison.

"Morning class," Principal York had smiled. "This is Felix Moon. It's his first day, so please make him feel welcome."

"Welcome, Felix. Take a seat over there, next to Sean," Mrs. Coolie had instructed.

I looked up at her thinking, *Who the hell is that?*

"Third row from the back," she'd said.

I'd nodded.

Then I'd walked up the aisle to the empty seat next to the window and sat down.

"Are you a vampire?" I had tilted my head towards the boy sat next to me. There was a head that popped out over his right shoulder. They were both looking at me like it was a serious question.

"Erm no, are you?" I didn't know what to say back, he'd asked if I was a vampire for Christ's sake.

"What about a werewolf?" said the head over his shoulder.

"Karl, don't be so silly," said Sean.

"I think it's equal to your vampire question, but now I'm not a werewolf nor am I a vampire. I'm just a normal human being," I'd replied.

"Not with those eyes, you're not just a human being," said Sean; and from that day on the three of us had become best friends. Not long after that, I had fallen out of the tree and got my wind power.

It was Star squeezing my hand so tightly that brought me back to reality. Calvin's eyes were still blood red, but they were shifting colour from red to blue then back again. It looked like he was fighting for control.

"Are you OK, Mr. Redfield?" asked Sean, moving away slowly.

"Mr. Redfield cannot come to the phone right now," said Calvin, with a creepy smile on his face.

"Dad, come back, please," Star whispered.

I had to do something, so I slowly started pulling his energy away from him. It was strange, as Calvin's energy felt

different; higher pitched and quicker. He looked over at me, tilted his head and said, "What do you think you are doing, boy?"

"Let Mr. Redfield come back and I will stop," I said defiantly.

"Do you know who I am? I'm Hellsolo Blood wolf and I can stop some puny third-rate witch," he sneered.

"That might be true, but I am no witch. I am a mod avatar and I can do what the hell I want!" I held both arms out with my hands like claws, facing him and I pulled his energy so fast it was making me feel dizzy. But he had so much power still left to get.

I felt a hand touch my arm. I didn't need to look. I knew it was Star because I felt the familiar little charge of energy between us. "Dad don't make me do this," she said quietly.

I stole a quick look at her. The tips of her hair were starting to turn red, a sign that she was storing too much power. "Star, what are you doing? Your hair is going red," I warned.

"It's OK, Felix. If Hellsolo Blood wolf is here, then Hellsolo Eden is coming out to play," she replied.

I didn't know what she was going on about until I looked at her for a second time. Her eyes had turned grey, just like mine. I was so confused by all of this.

"Well, well, well. Hellsolo Eden, what a pleasant surprise," said Calvin/Hellsolo Blood wolf, as he went down to his knees. He was fighting so hard to keep the remainder of his energy and I was getting lightheaded with so much power going through me.

"Hellsolo Blood wolf," Star said, addressing Calvin in a voice that sounded nothing like her own. Give Star her Father back, or else."

"Or else what? Hellsolo Eden, you forget I am stronger than you."

"That was true once, but with this young mod avatar sapping your energy, it is now *I* who is stronger than *you.*"

"NO!" he shouted. He tried to shoot me with a fireball, but I used my water possession to stop it in its tracks, with water from Kava's drink.

"Siste!" Star/Hellsolo Eden bellowed; and with one flick of her hand he was pinned up on the wall shouting in pain. She turned to me with those cold grey eyes and said, "Now Felix, take the rest of his power."

With that, I took the last of his power. The effort was too much, and I felt myself growing weak. "I think I need to lie down," I mumbled.

I closed my eyes and blacked out.

CHAPTER ELEVEN

The next thing I became aware of was muffled talking and someone playing with my hair. I flickered my eyes open to see a fuzzy Freddy.

"Fix, you still sleepy?" he asked.

"Not anymore, little man," I replied groggily.

"Phil, he's awake." I looked over to where my Mum's voice was coming from.

"Son, how are you? OK?" This was my Dad.

"Yes, thanks Dad. That was far too much energy for me."

"Are you hungry? You have been asleep for a long time," he said.

"I'm starving."

"I will make you some dinner. Come on Freddy, now you know he's woken up it's time for bed," said Mum.

"Night, Fix."

I helped him off the sofa and he ran to where mum was standing.

"Felix, someone would like to talk to you," Dad said, pointing to where Star was stood, but it wasn't really her, her eyes were still grey.

"Thank you, Mr. Moon. It was a pleasure to make your acquaintance," Hellsolo Eden said.

He just nodded and left. "Where is Star?" I demanded.

"She's here, look," and she pointed over to the mirror. I got up, still feeling dizzy and walked over to Star's reflection.

"She's not here. You give her back to me or I will do the same to you as I did to that other Hellsolo person!"

She came over and stood next to me. "Calm down, young mod avatar…look, there she is."

I looked back to the mirror and there she was, with her big brown eyes. I looked between the two of them – Star and Hellsolo Eden – one with brown eyes, one with grey eyes; and shivered. It gave me the creeps, how they could look so similar and yet be so different.

"Star, what's going on?" I said, looking in the mirror.

"Felix, this is my power priest, Hellsolo Eden."

"But why isn't she in the mirror?" I said, looking at Hellsolo Eden.

"She is inside me. This is the only way the three of us can talk. Felix, Hellsolo Eden wants to talk to you before I come back out. Please just remember, it's my body she's using, so don't hurt it."

"I would never hurt you," I said, putting my hand up to the mirror to touch her reflection.

"I know, but just keep it in mind," she said, reaching up to my hand in the mirror.

Hellsolo Eden and I went to sit on the sofa, opposite to where Calvin was sleeping.

"What did you want to talk about?" I asked, not trusting the power priest after what I'd seen Hellsolo Blood wolf was capable of.

"I just wanted to know if you are one of the good ones? In the past people have led her astray, me included." she smiled sadly, but it didn't reach her eyes...it was inhuman.

"I'm not like that. I love Star and I don't want anything to happen to her.

You on the other hand, you're the one pulling her in the wrong direction."

"That's not the case. I'm just like Star, I'm easily persuaded.

If it's what Star wants, I want to give it to her. I love her too, in my own way."

"So, we are on the same page. We both want to help Star, so all the formal stuff is over. How old are you? With the name Hellsolo Eden, I'm assuming you're female?"

She laughed at my silly question. "Well yes, I am female; and I am 547. I was born in 1468 and I died in 1495 when I was 27. My real name is Eden Gold," said Hellsolo Eden, looking down at her hands.

"How did you die?" I probed.

"I was hung for being a witch with the rest of my family, but with more powerful witches and warlocks like myself, we can stay on this astral realm. We can become Hellsolo's and be absorbed by a young witch or warlock when they reach the age of 12. Star is different though. I've been with her since she was nine."

That was the same age I was when I fell out of the tree and took possession of the wind power, coincidence? I think not. With my life the way it is now, I don't believe in coincidences anymore. *I will have to ask her,* I thought. "How come you were able to possess Star so young?" I said.

"Well, for a start, her royal blood is intoxicating to Hellsolo's and –"

"Royal?" I interrupted.

"Yes, Star is a Princess of the magic realm. Didn't you know?"

"No...I didn't," I said, confused.

"Prince Calvin was stripped of his title when he married Annadora. That's probably why she never told... you. Hang on...she never knew. I can hear her talking in my head. Star didn't know about being a royal. He – Calvin that is – told her she was just special; and that it was why she was possessed by me so young. I'm so sorry Star, I didn't know you never knew," Hellsolo Eden said to herself.

"So, where do we go from here?" I asked, but there was no response.

"Eden? You OK?" I touched her arm.

"Sorry, yes, I'm fine, but Star...not so much."

"Can I speak to her? Please?"

"Of course, you can. It was lovely to finally meet you in person, Felix."

"And you too, Eden."

"It's strange, just being called Eden after spending so many years as a Hellsolo. I like it." She smiled and, for just a second, I swear I caught a glimpse of the person she used to be when she was alive.

"Well, it's your name, isn't it? A Hellsolo is *what* you are, not *who* you are," I said, returning her smile.

She closed her eyes and tilted her head back, so it was facing the ceiling.

After a minute or two she put her hands over her face and started crying.

"Star?" I checked.

She nodded.

I put my arms around her to comfort her. "I can't believe they never told me," she sobbed.

"They might have thought it was for the best at the time," I said gently.

"For the best? For the best for who? I still should have been told. To have such a strong and powerful entity inside me so young, it was hard, the fight for control," she said. She shook her head, remembering the struggle.

"I don't understand. Why did they not tell you? What is it about your royalty that makes Hellsolo's want to possess you?" I said, trying to understand.

"Being a royal means, you attract more powerful Hellsolo's. It's hard to explain," she said, searching for the right words before continuing. "Think of this way. Normal witches get like, a level one to four Hellsolo, but royals get a level five Hellsolo, whether they like it or not. If my parents had just told me, I could have been more prepared for it."

"I'm sorry, Star," I said, hugging her tighter.

It was late when Star and Chadwick took Calvin home. He was still unconscious, and I felt bad because I'd taken so much power from him. I can still feel the last little bits of his power flowing through me. It burns, like eating something hot and spicy.

I ate the sausage and mash that my Mum made for me, then said goodnight and went to bed; stopping first at Freddy's room to check on him. He was sound asleep.

Walking into my room, it was pitch black. I didn't turn the light on, as I was just going to flop on my bed and sleep in my clothes, but something wasn't right. It felt wrong. I used my wind power to push the light switch on and there, in the corner of the room, a woman was standing looking at me. Needless to say, I was freaked out.

"Erm, hello?" I said.

I looked at her face again as I got up off my bed. It looks familiar, but I'm not sure where from.

"So, you're Felix? You're the one that's going to kill me?" she said, a smirk on her face.

My eyes widened. *Holy crap!* "Annadora," I breathed.

"The one and only," she said, doing a little twirl.

I heard a noise from behind me. Looking around, I saw Kayos. He had Karl in in bear-hug, with one hand over his mouth.

'No, no, no, no, no, no, no,' I said, over and over again. I've tried so hard to stop this from happening. "Please don't do this! We can work something out," I tried to plead.

"But it's been foreseen. I don't come out well on the other side of this battle," Annadora said.

I was looking between Annadora and Kayos. Do I tell them that it's not true? Do I tell them that Chadwick has his foresight back? Looking into Karl's eyes, I tried to find answers to my questions. Karl shook his head; he had answered my silent question.

"You're going to die Annadora," I spat at her. "The same goes for you Kayos. I'm going to kill you both. You killed me and got me trapped in Alicade for nearly *seven years*!"

"You forget Felix," Kayos drawled. "I was stuck there too."

"Yeah and who's fault was that? You broke the portal, the only way in and out of Alicade."

Kayos had a stupid smirk on his face that I wanted to punch off. I balled up my fists. "Go," Annadora said, I was confused at first. I looked over at Annadora; then Kayos said, "Goodbye, Felix." I looked back over to where he had been standing, but he was gone and so was Karl. My heart sank to my feet. All I could think was, *I've failed him, I couldn't save him.*

"You bring Karl back *right now* or so help me god!"

"And what is *your god* going to do? Huh? Nothing!" Annadora laughed, it was a cruel sound. "I might bring him back, but first, you might know where something of mine is. It's about this big and it's red and white; looks like a crystal."

I knew exactly what she was after and where it was. Her Crybecker. It was in my left trouser pocket. After Aries had told me what was; and how much power it gives Annadora, I'd made sure it had never left my side. "I don't know what you are talking about?" I bluffed.

"Now Felix, I know that's not true. Your Great Grandfather Felix stole it from me, and I want it back!"

"What, so you can go around killing more avatars? No thanks."

"No, not just avatars...everyone that defies me," she said, as if the lives of others meant nothing to her. "I'm going to rule everything, this world, and all the others."

She sounded so full of herself. *Others?* I didn't dwell on it. I laughed. "Not going to happen, love. Not while I'm still breathing."

In the blink of an eye Annadora was stood in front of me, with her hand around my neck. "Don't tempt me, boy. I could do it, you know," she whispered.

"And you know that I'm a mod avatar. I can take your energy away."

"But you won't, because I have something you want. Poor Karl, I'd just *hate it* if something bad were to happen to him. I think we can make a trade."

"I still don't know what you're talking about," I said, trying not to think about Karl.

"Come on, Felix. I know you know what it is and where to find it. I will give you…one week to find it and return it to me, or you can say goodbye to your friend forever and you won't ever find him."

I nodded and she let go of my throat. "Goodbye Felix…until Friday."

Then Annadora ran to the open window and jumped out headfirst.

CHAPTER TWELVE

I just stood there for hours, time escaped me. I was helpless. I needed to save my friend, but at the same time, I don't want to give Annadora her Cry becker either. *Maybe I should speak to my great Grandfather for help,* I thought, but he doesn't know that Chadwick has his foresight back.

It was light outside now, but I hadn't noticed; I was too busy trying to come up with a solution to my problem.

There was a little tap at the door. "Felix, Karl, are you boys hungry?"

"Mum…" I started to say.

She must have heard the pain in my voice because she burst straight through the door. "What's the matter?"

I was silent, tears rolling down my face. "Felix, why are you crying?" Mum asked, putting her arms around me.

"Felix, where's Karl?"

"Mum. He's. Gone." I said, between sobs.

"Gone? What do you mean gone?"

"When I went to bed last night, Annadora and Kayos were waiting for me in here. They took him and I couldn't save him."

"Took him? They've kidnapped him! Why didn't you come straight to us?"

"Oh Mum, there's so much I haven't told you about all of this. I didn't want you to worry about me. I just don't know if I can handle it anymore. I just want my normal life back," I said, still crying.

"Oh Felix, sit down and tell me everything."

So, I told her everything. I couldn't stop once I'd started. I told her all about having to die to get my powers, all about getting stuck in Alicade and my mission to kill (or save) Annadora.

After I'd told her everything, it felt like there was a little weight lifted off my shoulders. No more secrets. "Mum, you OK?"

"Erm yes, I think I will be fine. It's just a lot of information to take in. Let's go downstairs and get everyone here and we can all talk about it."

We gathered everyone around the kitchen table for some lunch and I told them that Annadora and Kayos had taken Karl. They were all shocked into silence. I let it sink in before hitting them with another blow, by telling them that it's Karl who gets killed by Annadora. Star already knew about Karl, but she still started crying, as did my Mum. Dad was consoling her. Red and Ben just shook their heads in disbelieve. Chadwick already knew my plan. Sean had his hands over his face so I couldn't see his reaction to the news, but I could feel in his energy that he was devastated. I also told them about my plan: to give everyone a power who wanted one, even Karl. "How were you going to give a power to

Karl? He didn't want one the last time you asked. Why do you think he would take one off you now?" asked Sean.

"I don't know Sean. Pin him down and force it on him. He drowns Sean! I need to save him. I can't let him die that way. This is all my fault, I should have stayed in Alicade and not come back," I said, pushing my chair back so hard it tipped over. I walked straight out of the front door; I needed time to think, to clear my head.

I found myself in the town's graveyard, standing in front of my own grave. Someone had put my coffin back in the ground and covered it with grass so it didn't look like I had just popped out of it.

I sat on the ground, looking up at my gravestone, reading it over and over again:

In loving memory of

Felix Michael Moon

A loving son, brother and friend

I sat there for a while, until I felt a big, thick energy behind me that I recognised. "Hey Kava," I said without looking.

"Felix," he replied, sitting down beside me. "What's this?" Kava said, pointing at the headstone.

"This is where I was buried when I got stuck in Alicade. They thought I was dead and not coming back."

"But you are not dead, so why is your grave still here?"

"Everyone still thinks I'm dead. Just the people closest to me know I'm not."

"Can I speak my mind?" asked Kava.

"You never need to ask for permission to speak. You're not in Alicade now," I said, putting my hand on his shoulder.

"What is wrong with you?"

"What do you mean?" I asked.

"Ever since you brought me here," Kava started, "I've noticed that you are different. You are a lot more tense, more emotional. When you left Alicade you were so headstrong, a soldier. You didn't take no for an answer. If someone told you no, you still went and did whatever you wanted to do...you were a leader, Felix. You act so differently around these people."

"These people are my family and friends and I cannot be that person around them."

"Am I not your friend?" Kava said, in a low voice full of sadness.

"Of course, you are, we spent nearly seven years fighting together, but these are just humans. They have no power in this fight unless I give it to them. They are so fragile," I said, shaking my head.

"OK, I think I understand now. But think of this, Felix. If you get too emotionally evolved, you will make mistakes that could cost you dearly. Come on my friend, let's go and get your other friend back," Kava said, getting up and holding his hand out for me. I took it and jumped up.

We walked the long way home through the woods because it was too risky for me to walk out in the open. After a while, I could sense someone behind us. I glanced behind a few times, but I didn't see anything. "Kava. I think someone is following us," I whispered. He just nodded and we split up; I carried on walking forward and Kava broke off to the left. I slowed my pace so as not to leave the woods.

"FELIX!" I heard Kava shout.

I quickly turned and felt for his energy and ran towards it. When I reached him, I got the shock of my life. I would never have guessed who the person following us had been; the person whom Kava currently had by the throat. "Mrs. Hardy!"

I couldn't believe my eyes. It was Sean's Mother. Sean had told me that she had died a few months after I had. I repeated, "Mrs. Hardy?"

"Felix," she struggled to say.

"Kava, let her go!"

He did as he was told. He let go of her neck, but he still had a hold of her forearm. "Felix, I can explain," said Mrs. Hardy.

"I think you need to talk fast," I said, getting angry.

"I faked my death," she said simply.

"Why?" I snapped.

She shook her head, not wanting to tell me.

Kava said, "I don't think you have much of a choice, madam. Felix and I are very powerful."

"I know. She told me as much," mumbled Mrs. Hardy.

"Who told you?" I said, stepping forward. Silence. "WHO?" I shouted. She flinched, but still, she was silent. "Don't make me mad, Mrs. Hardy. I've had the worst few days, so don't test me," I said, my hands shaking. I could feel the anger building inside me, and I could feel the fire running through my veins. The ground began to shake beneath our feet.

"Felix, you have to understand. I had to do it to save my family!"

"Then tell me why?" I roared.

"Annadora," Mrs. Hardy spat the name like it was poison. "She wanted my power of foresight. She wanted to know what is going happen to her, but I can't see it.

It keeps changing when it shouldn't."

I was shocked. Mrs. Hardy had powers? I hid the surprise from my voice. "What do you mean, changing?" I asked.

"There's someone called Calvin. He keeps changing his mind. She wouldn't tell me who he was. She tried killing me, but I got away then faked my death so she wouldn't look for me. I never went

too far. I kept going into my garden at night, to see my boys.
Then, one night, I was sitting in the garden and I saw you come in
and talk to Sean. You were supposed to be dead, like me. I really
thought you were going to see me."

"So, you have powers then? How did I not know that? I should
have been able to sense it," I said, looking away.

"Who's Calvin?" I didn't hear her question, I was busy feeling for
her energy, and there it was. Her energy felt similar to
Chadwick's. I'm guessing that's because they have the same
power.

"So, if you have the power of foresight, then you
should have known we were going to capture you," said Kava,
snapping me out of my daze.

"I couldn't see. My powers are weak. The boy tried to take my
power away."

"How?" I asked.

"With magic, but I got away before he took it all."

"Who tried to take your powers?"

"I can't remember his name."

"Was it Kayos?"

"Yes, that's it."

"You're lying. Kayos was stuck in Alicade with us then, it was after
he broke the portal."

"I'm not lying, he was there. Annadora was possessing someone."

"That *someone* was my baby brother Freddy. But if he was there with you, then how did he get between worlds with no portal?" I knew she wasn't lying now. I had my emotions under control. How did he get back and forth with no portal? Spell maybe? I'd have to ask Star when I got back. I'd need to look in Baltazar's journal as well.

"How did you get away?" Kava said, breaking my concentration again. I really needed to stop zoning out.

"I pretended to pass out when a man brought my food," Mrs. Hardy explained. "Then, when he came over to help me, I stabbed him with the fork and ran. I didn't know where I was going, but I didn't care. I just wanted to get out of there. When I ran, it was so cold. I had no shoes on, but I kept on running until I found a road. I don't know how long I walked along the road before someone finally stopped. They took me to the next pit stop. I felt terrible when I stole their car and left them there, but I had to come back here. I couldn't just show up, Annadora and the boy – Kayos – might have been watching for me, so I faked my death and stayed in the basement at night."

"You know that I can give you back your power of foresight?" I asked.

"I don't want it back," she said. "All it has brought me is pain and misery. You can take it away, I don't care."

She took me off guard for a minute. I thought she would have wanted it back. "I'm not going to take it off you, just in case you change your mind. It's not an easy process for me to give it back."

"What shall we do with her, Felix?" asked Kava.

"I don't know, let me think for a second," I said, but my head was swimming with her story.

What to do, what to do? She is my best friend's Mum, after all. Do I let her go and make Kava swear not to tell, or do I take her back to the house? Sean will obviously see her if I do the latter, but I can't not tell him that his Mother is alive. Nothing ever ends well when I keep secrets.

"Mrs. Hardy...what to do with you? Go back to being 'dead' or come back with us, but be warned, I will tell Sean that you're alive either way," I said.

I could see the shocked look on Kava's face.

"But if I go back, Sean will see me. What will I tell him?"

"The truth," Kava said.

"But I'm meant to be dead."

"So am I," I laughed; and continued, "And he took it well. To be honest, he's watched me die four times now and that's not including the times I go to Alicade. I think he will be fine. He will be a little emotional, but fine."

"OK Felix, take me back to my son."

CHAPTER THIRTEEN

On the way back to the house Mrs. Hardy was telling us what Annadora was getting her to look for, but me being me, I zoned out again. What Kava had said to me has really struck a chord. I do need to start to think like the leader that I know I am. I will have to do what needs to be done, not what everyone else wants me to do. No one will like it, but I am the mod avatar after all.

I flashed back to when I was in Alicade. I must have only been there a year or so when I was promoted to second in command. I was promoted after Kava and I broke rank and disobeyed the then head of the guards, Captain Javan.

I didn't like him and he knew it, but I think the feeling was a mutual one. He thought that we should just stay back at the portal and keep it safe, but I knew that we needed to push the invaders back to the borders of the palace; so, Kava and I hatched a plan to do just that.

I attacked head on and Kava from the left, it didn't take too long. There were only about thirty of Kayos's men. Not to blow my own trumpet, but we killed it. I did end up with a broken collar bone, and Kava with four broken ribs and a punctured lung, but the witches healed us up nicely.

Javan was livid. He suspended us with immediate effect. Well, that is until King Brogue came to see us.

"Felix Jr, Kava. Are you both OK?" he'd asked.

"Yes, we're good. Nothing a witch or two can't fix," I'd joked.

"But seriously, Jr, you could have been killed; and killed Kava along with you. Don't you think you were reckless and unthinking of others safety?"

"Well, someone has to be. I've been fighting for nearly a year and just sitting back defending the portal gives Kayos and his men the advantage, but now they have been pushed back past the Black Fountain," I'd said.

"Don't you think you should have brought it up with Captain Javan?" the King has enquired.

I could see Capt. Javan behind the King, looking a little worried, but I wouldn't crap all over him; as much as I don't like him. I couldn't do it. "No, I didn't.

I just told Kava and we went," I'd replied, shaking my head. I could see Kava's look of disapproval.

"I have to admit his skill while defending Kava was second to none, but his offensive skills are lacking," Captain Javan had supplied.

"OK Jr, what if I promote you to second in command?"

"But sire," Capt. Javan had said, incredulous. "I have suspended them for reckless abandonment of their posts. What if their little solo mission had failed? There was a gap in the wall. Kayos's army could have broken through and –"

"ENOUGH!" King Brogue had boomed. "What I say is final. Jr, you are second in command, with Kava as your direct reporting officer."

I couldn't help but be a little smug when Capt. Javan looked over at me.

Back in the real world, we had reached home and I had a clearer head on my shoulders. I left Kava and Mrs. Hardy out in the back garden and went inside. I pulled Sean into the living room.

"OK, Sean...I erm...have something to tell you, but I know you can take it," I told him.

"Felix, what are you going on about? You're starting to freak me out," I said.

I did have to laugh to myself. With all that we have gone through, my sitting him down to talk to him is freaking him out. "I wanted to ask you a question? When I came back from the 'dead', how did you feel?" I said, trying to keep my emotions off my face.

"Felix, where is this going?" Sean said, confused.

"Just answer the question."

"I don't know, all kinds of things, but most of all I felt relief. I had missed you so much. After my Mother died, you were the one I wanted to see. As much as I had Karl and Star, you're the one who I felt would understand."

There was a long pause as I tried to find the right words. "OK, Sean…Sean…erm…" I didn't know how to say it, to tell him that his Mother was still alive.

"Felix, just spit it out!"

"How would you feel if I told you that your Mum was outside in the back garden with Kava?" OK, so that could have come out better.

Sean just stared at me with wide eyes then, slowly, he stood up.

"If this is some sort of sick joke, Felix, I'm going to kill you."

"Sean, you know I wouldn't do that. She's been following us for a while."

Sean said nothing as he headed to the back door, with me close behind. He walked quickly through the kitchen past the others, who were all there. I held up my hand to everyone to signal them to stay put and then carried on out of the back door with Sean. It was a beautiful moment between them, hugging and crying. Kava and I left them outside to talk. Walking back into the kitchen, I apologised to the others for my actions before, when I ran out like a little baby, but they understood. They know all about the weight that is on my shoulders. Sometimes it's good to let off some steam.

That night I couldn't get to sleep. All I could think of was Karl being kidnapped by Annadora and Kayos and how he must be so scared; so, I decided to read Baltazar's journal to distract me from everything.

Before I could open the book there was a knock at the door.

"Come in," I called out.

It was Kava who walked through the door. "Felix, I have been thinking, we need to talk," he said.

"Of course, my friend. What do you want to talk about?"

"The fact that you are working with Annadora's children – how well do you know them? How do you know they are not going to sell you out? You gave Chadwick back his powers; how do you know for a fact that he is telling the truth?"

He spoke quickly. I knew this was hard for him to say to me.

"Kava, I know you're looking out for me, but I've known them longer than you have. They have told me their stories."

"That's just it, Felix...' stories'. How do you know they're true?"

"I know they're telling the truth. I know when people are lying to me. I think it's the energy power that I possess. Plus, I have a special connection to Star. I trust them. If you don't, then put your trust in me, Kava. I am your friend, so please, just trust that I know what I am doing," I said, putting my hand on his shoulder.

"So, what is the plan?"

"Erm, to be honest, I have no clue. I was going to look in Baltazar's journal to see if I can get any ideas." I laughed, sitting back on my bed and picking up the journal.

I had been looking through the book for what felt like hours. Kava was still in my room. He was at the computer looking on Google. He was looking up all the things he'd missed in the time he had been dead in this world.

As I read, I came to a part of the book that talked about avatars. Just the run of the mill avatars, the ones that only possess one of the elements: earth, wind, fire or water. Balthazar has written that they have a weak spot, that when they are conjuring their element, they are vulnerable.

I had assumed that an avatar could be killed just like any other person. I know my Granddad died of old age, so I'd thought that avatars would be vulnerable to the same dangers as normal people. Apparently, you can't *kill* an avatar in any normal way, but they can get *wounded* in the normal way. I'd never even thought of asking Kava how he died.

"Kava, can I ask you a question?" I asked.

Kava looked up from the computer, where he had been reading about Game of Thrones. "Of course, you can, boss. Anything," he replied.

"You don't have to answer if you don't want to but...how did you die?" "Erm, well it was a long time ago, but it happened when I was fighting for my King. He knew I had 'special powers', so I gave him the upper hand in a fight, but we had a...disagreement."

"What kind of disagreement?" I asked. I could see that Kava was getting unconformable. "It's OK if you don't want to tell me."

"Its fine, it happened a long time ago and I serve my true King now, King Brogue."

If only he knew the truth, I thought. I don't know if I should tell him or not. Only Chadwick and I knew about Chadwick's vision of me being crowned as Alicade's King.

Kava continued, "King Favian – my former ruler – listened to the wrong person. There was this advisor called Tyrian. I thought I'd just found him now, on this Game of Thrones thing, but it wasn't him."

"Kava, you're getting off topic."

"Sorry. Well, Tyrion persuaded the King to go to war with the Lincain Kingdom, across the Fain Sea. King Lincain was a peaceful man; we never had any trouble from him until Tyrion arrived. He said he was from the Lincain Kingdom and that the Lincain's were going to start a war with King Favian. He told Favian he needed to strike first. I said it was a bad idea and then I was banished to the wall at the water's edge."

"Kava, I'm going to ask a stupid question, but here goes. Were you born on this earth? All the people you have mentioned, all these places, I've never heard of them."

Kava looked at me, puzzled. "Of course, I was born here. This is Earth Nova, after all?"

"Earth what?"

"Earth Nova. Felix, why are you looking at me like that?"

"Kava, this planet is just called Earth, not Earth Nova. As far as we know, there is only one planet that supports life."

"Really?" Kava said, spinning his chair back to the computer. He started Googling 'earth nova', but nothing was coming up. "I don't understand, why can't find anything?" he said, getting frustrated and slamming his fists on the desk.

"Shush Kava," I hissed. "People are asleep in the house. Just finish your story and we can talk after."

Kava nodded and turned back towards me. I could see he was upset, but he tried to hide it. He coughed and carried on his story. "At the wall, I had a lot of time to think and one night, I took a boat out across the Fain Sea. I wanted to talk to King Lincain. When we spoke, he told me that Tyrion had done the same to him; trying to convince him that King Favian was going to war with him, but King Lincain had none of it and kicked him out the Kingdom."

"Then why didn't King Lincain send a message to King...?" I had forgotten the unfamiliar name.

"King Favian...he did, but we never got it. Turns out Tyrion killed the messenger."

"So, how did you die?"

"I told my King and I was executed for treason," Kava said simply.

"But in Baltazar's book, it says you can't kill an avatar in any normal way?"

"Well, they cut off my head then I woke up in Alicade."

"Wow, that's quite a story. Thanks for telling me, Kava." I said, and I meant it I knew it must have been hard for him to tell me.

"Is that everything? I'm kind of beat."

"Yes, thanks Kava, you may leave."

Kava left, but I was far from tired. I should have been, as I've had next to no sleep in the last few days. I felt like I needed to get Kava some answers, so a quick trip to Alicade wouldn't hurt. Everyone was asleep and I would be back before dawn, so nobody would realise where I had gone.

I laid down and thought about Falkor, the big throne room, and King Brogue's dark green throne.

When I arrived in Alicade I was in the throne room, just as I had imagined I would be, but it was quiet, and no one was around. It was night-time, so there would usually be a guard still walking around, but there was no one. It was eerie.

"Hello?" I shouted. There was no reply.

I went to the door and it was locked. I didn't know that the door could lock. I jiggled the door handle to try and get out but to no avail. So, what could I do? I took a seat on the throne. It was not comfortable at all. It got me thinking though, about what would happen if I did become King? King Felix. I don't think I would like the pressure that it comes with that title.

I'm only...how old am I? I'm 22, no I'm only 17 in the other world. Oh my god, this is so confusing what with the time difference.

It was starting to get light outside, and I still hadn't seen anyone, but now I could hear a noise coming from behind the throne. I just sat there, waiting to see who it was. "Felix! What are you doing? Get off my throne!"

Jani. I groaned inwardly; he was the last person I wanted to see.

"Jani, this is not your throne. Where is the King?" I demanded to know.

"He is...away," Jani said, with that stupid smirk on his stupid face. I hate this man.

"Away? Away where?"

"It's none of your business, I'm the one in charge now."

"I don't think, so my ugly friend. Where is my great Granddad?"

Suddenly, he lunged at me, but I was ready. It was easy to use my wind power against him. I pushed him away and pinned him up on the wall. Jani looked at me, shocked. "How are you doing that?" he sputtered.

"Doing what? Using my powers?"

"Yes, the throne is laced with voodoo magic. Nobody can use their powers in here."

"I'm a mod avatar! That makes me the highest-ranking person in this room. Now tell me, where is my Granddad?" I said, tightening the wind around his neck.

"Not…telling…you," Jani struggled to say.

I clicked my fingers and a bright orange flame appeared. "Jani, I'm giving you one last chance to tell me. I'm already having the worst week of my life, so tell me where the King and my Granddad are, or I will set you alight."

He still stayed quiet, so I moved the flame closer to his face, still nothing. I gave him another warning, nothing, so I let the flame touch his face. "Ahhhh, stop, stop, stop," he cried out in pain. "Where are they?"

"Ok, I will tell you," Jani said. I blew out the flame. "Where?" I barked. Jani put his hand to where I had burned him. The smell wasn't too pleasant, but he'd had plenty of warnings, right? "Where?" I repeated my question. "They're both in the dungeon vault," he spat. "The dungeon? What the hell have you done Jani?" I let him down but still had the wind wrapped around his neck. "Take me to them, NOW!"

Jani unlocked the door and we left the throne room.

The dungeon was across the courtyard. As soon as we got outside, I could feel Jani building up his power, so I forcefully pulled his energy away from him, leaving him nearly powerless. Three guards were stood in the middle of the courtyard.

"Guards," Jani shouted. They turned; and before I knew what was happening, a ball of fire rushed past my face. I sent Jani up in the air and froze him in place there.

"Hey guys, it's me, Felix," I said hopefully. Another ball of fire came shooting towards me, but this time I was ready. I sent water hurtling out of my left hand, while clicking my right fingers to let the fire light up my whole arm. "Gent's we are friends, not enemies. It's Jani we should be fighting."

"Put King Jani down," one of the guards ordered.

"King Jani? He is no King. King Brogue and my Granddad are in the dungeon." I noticed that each of the three guards had a black mark on the right side of their neck.

I remembered reading about those marks in a book in the King's library. I'd read that when someone is touched by black magic, it appears as a black mark on the neck.

"Ok listen, you have been touched by black magic. You don't know what's right or wrong. I'm telling you the truth. Jani has lied to you."

But before I could finish my sentence, something hit me from behind and I went flying down the steps. I hit the ground hard. I nearly lost my concentration on Jani. He fell a few feet before I pushed him back up. That was the last straw! I lost it. I balled my fists and hit the ground. It started rumbling and then the earth opened up underneath the three guards, and they fell down the hole I'd created.

I quickly got up and ran up the steps, dodging more fire balls. I grabbed the guard around the neck, picked him up and threw him over my shoulder. He slammed into the steps and cried out in pain.

Side note: since I've become a full mod avatar, I can feel myself getting stronger. Slinging this guard and slamming him to the ground, it was like I'd picked up Freddy.

Ok, back to the fight, or not. It's not fair to them really. I'm a hell of a lot stronger than they are. I grabbed the guard by the scruff of his neck and chucked him down the crater I'd made. Now there were four of them down there. I didn't want to kill them; it wasn't their fault that they had black magic in them.

I looked back to where Jani was, still high in the air. I pulled him closer to where I was standing then took the wind away. Jani fell. He hit the floor with a crack. "Ouch, my arm," he moaned. "I think it's broken!"

"Oh, what a shame, Jani," I said sarcastically. "Jump down in the hole, there's a good boy."

"I'm not getting in there."

I grabbed him and said, "You either jump down there, or I will push you so far down into that hole that you won't come ever out of it. Well, not alive anyway. Your choice."

He took too long to decide, so I made the ground start to shake again. "Alright, alright, I'll jump."

I pushed him closer to the edge and he jumped. I walked over and looked down at him. "Comfy down there?" I joked.

I put an energy layer over the hole. If someone tried to go through it, they'd get zapped of energy. And anyone with one of those black marks on their neck wouldn't be able to get out.

By the time I got to the other side of the courtyard, I'd trapped 17 people in the hole. I was impressed with myself.

At the gate to the stables (the dungeon was located underneath), there was a young guard. I remembered him from when I was stuck here, all those Alicade years ago.

What was his name? I racked my brain, trying to think of what his name was. "Do you know who I am?" I asked as I approached him.

I could see he was nervous, and he was shaking. I could just about see his black mark. It wasn't very dark in colour, like the other guard's marks had been. "Yes," he replied curtly. "You're Felix Moon, but you look different, younger."

"You can see what's going on here. You're going to let me through with no trouble at all," I said calmly.

The young guard raised his hand. There was already had a rather large water orb in it, it had started to freeze over. "I can't stop it,

Felix. I don't want to hurt you. I'm sorry," the young guard said, as the ball of ice came towards me.

I just dodged it. Wow, this boy was fast! Before I knew it, three more ice orbs came shooting towards me. Two of them went straight passed me, but the third hit me square in the chest. It took the wind out of me and I fell to my knees, clutching my chest. "Sorry," the young guard said, "but I can't fight it anymore. I can feel it taking me over."

"It's…ok…kid…I… know…it's…not…you. I…can…help…you," I said, breathing after every word. My chest hurt. I know I said earlier that I was a lot stronger than everyone here, but the speed that his ice orb came at me was unexpected. I put my hand out in front of me and started to pull his energy away.

"What's happening? What are you doing?" the kid said. In that moment he sounded very young, and very scared.

"Just relax and try not to hurt me."

After a few seconds, the boy's head fell forward. I quickly got up through the pain and grabbed the young guard before he hit the floor. I dragged the lad just inside the gates. "*Bruno!* Bruno Sparks, that's his name," I blurted out to myself.

Walking down the stairs to the dungeon, I'm not going to lie, it was creepy down there; and why does it have to be so dirty?

"King Brogue? Granddad?" I called out.

"Felix Jr," said King Brogue's voice.

"Where are you?" I said. It was so dark that I couldn't even see my hand in front of my face.

I could just make out a hand coming out of one of the cell bars. I raced over to the hand. Looking into the cell, I could only see King Brogue. "Where's my Granddad?"

"He's down here. He's not in a good way, we can't get out. The lock has been laced with voodoo magic."

"I have no problem with that," I said, putting my hand over the lock and flooding it with water; then freezing it. It didn't take long before the lock broke. I opened the cell door to a stunned King Brogue, but I ignored him and went straight to my Granddad. He was asleep on a bed of straw.

"How did you do that, Jr?" Brogue asked.

"I'm a mod avatar. I don't think there's anything that can stop my powers. What happened to my Granddad?"

"There was an issue at the Glacier that needed our urgent attention. Once we arrived back, World War Eight had kicked off –"

I had to interrupt, saying, "World War 8?"

"Time works differently here, you know that. It could be years here between your visits, but that's getting off topic. When we got back, we discovered that Jani had used black magic on the guards. They jumped our wagon. Your Granddad got hurt defending me and we have been down here for weeks."

"Don't worry, King Brogue. Everything is about to change."

I moved to the middle of the cell. "Felix Jr, what are you doing?"

"Just wait and see. It will amaze you."

I tried to relax and fill my head with Star's energy. I felt for our connection and let it flow through me until it disappeared. I opened my eyes and there she was. I didn't acknowledge her, I just closed my eyes again and did the same with Sean, Ben, Red, Chadwick, and Kava.

I tried to feel for Karl's energy as well, on the off chance it would work, it didn't.

Once I had finished, the cell was getting a little cramped and loud.

"What the hell was that?" Sean said, rubbing his head in confusion.

"Granddad!" Red exclaimed, rushing past me, closely followed by Ben.

"Felix, why is the King in the dungeon?" This came from Kava.

"Jani," I said.

"That little weasel, I'm going to kill him," Kava replied.

"Kava, my dear friend, it's been a while," King Brogue said, putting his hand on Kava's shoulder.

"Felix, how did you do this?" asked Sean.

"The same way I got Kava to the real world. I pulled you through the portal."

"It was weird. It felt like I was spinning out of control. Is that what it's like for you?"

"Yeah, and it's something you don't get used to. Ok, we can do all the questions later, but right now Jani has control of Alicade. He and a few guards are in a hole in the courtyard, but I know when we leave there will be an army out there. Do you think you are ready to fight?"

"But I don't have any powers," Sean said quietly.

"I can give you power," I said. "But you have no time to train, so you will stay here with my Granddad and protect him. I can give you the wind element; it's the easiest one to possess. You had it once before, so you know the basics of the power. I will still put an energy field around you too, to protect you as best I can."

"And I will put a spell over the cell, so it's hard for them to find you," Star said.

So, I gave Sean the wind power. "Wow Felix, it feels so weird, like before," Sean said as he made a wind orb in his hand.

"Jr, how can you do that?" said King Brogue, amazed.

"The same reason I can bring everyone here. I'm a mod avatar," I replied.

"Just amazing," he said and then he went to see Granddad Felix. He was out of earshot then, so I turned to Star and asked, "Star, the guards have been touched with black magic. Is there any way you could help with that?"

"No, I can't. But…"

"Hellsolo Eden?" I whispered. "Yep." "Will she help?" I asked, worried. "I think she will."

"No Star don't do it. You know it's a bad idea." I thought back to what I had been told; that once, Hellsolo Eden had taken Star over and was able to control her. I did not want that to happen again.

"How else can I remove the black mark? She's the only one with the power to remove it," Star said, walking over to Chadwick.

"But what if she takes you over?" I asked.

"She won't. She didn't last time. She wants what I want."

"But…" Chadwick began.

"Sorry Chadwick, but it's the only way."

Star closed her eyes and said, "Hellsolo Eden, I need your help." Her head fell backwards, and she started chanting in Latin.

"Star! Are you ok?" I asked, getting closer to her. Then she opened her eyes and looked at me, and I knew it wasn't her anymore. The silver eyes of Star's Hellsolo were looking back at me. "Hello Eden," I said, by way of greeting.

"Hello Felix, how have you been?" she replied, in that unfamiliar voice of hers.

"I've been good, you?"

"What the hell is going on? Just go remove the mark that's on the guards, then give Star back," said Chadwick, getting angry.

"Chadwick, I'm not like that anymore. I just wanted to give Star what she wants. She wanted to be with her Mother back then, so I give it to her. Now she wants to be with Felix, and I will do what she wants. I will remove the mark then I will leave," Eden explained all this in a tone that said she thought that what she was saying was obvious.

"You will just go back inside, but not leave her? Right," I said.

"No, I won't leave her...I couldn't even if I wanted to. I'm only released when the host dies."

It's strange, I'm drawn to Star, but with Hellsolo Eden it's even stronger. I don't want her to leave Star because then I wouldn't see her again. I know it's wrong, but the connection feels stronger with Hellsolo Eden. Do you think it's Eden I'm more attracted to? I don't know myself.

We started talking about how we were going to take Falkor back. Sean and Chadwick are going to stay with my Granddad, while Red and Ben will go up the left side of the courtyard. King Brogue and Star will go up to the right and Kava and I will go straight up the middle to try to draw them to me.

Red and Ben were the first people to the doors of Falkor. "Just go," I shouted, as I threw another guard into the pit.

The courtyard was clear, so I told King Brogue and Kava to stay with Hellsolo Eden while she starts removing the black magic from the guards. I went into Falkor to try and find the others. I felt for their energy. "Crap, they've split up," I said aloud to myself.

I decided to follow Ben. His energy felt more active, so I realised he must have been fighting.

He wasn't too far away I could see he was fighting off three guards. He was fighting well. Between us, we got them down and out for the count. "Why did you two split up?" I asked. "You should have stayed together."

"You lot were busy outside, and we were ready to go in. We just thought that if we split up, we could take this place before we needed help."

"It looks like you've been practicing with your power, I'm impressed," I said, patting Ben on the shoulder.

"Come on, let's go find Red," Ben said.

"Ok one sec, let me feel for him."

"You what?" Ben said, confused.

"I can feel a person's energy. It's part of being a mod avatar. It's how I knew you were fighting, your energy felt faster than it normally does."

"Oh right. Well then, feel away creepy boy."

I rolled my eyes and felt for Red's energy. "Found him, he's this way," I said; and we were off.

We found Red in the throne room with a guard that had a knife to his throat. "Red!" Ben shouted. I could feel the rage bubbling up inside, the fire flowing through my veins.

"Felix, I've heard a lot about you," the guard said.

"All bad I hope," I quipped.

"Felix, don't piss him off," Ben warned, then he turned to Red's captor and said, "Just put the knife down and we can talk."

"Sorry, I do not know who you are," the guard said.

"I'm Felix's brother, so just let Red go. Felix, *do something!*"

"There is nothing he can do. His powers do not work in this room."

"You want to bet on that?" I said, letting the flames loose so that they engulfed both my hands.

"What the…" said the guard, holding the knife closer to Red's throat.

"Put the knife down now and you won't get hurt," I said.

At that moment King Brogue appeared from behind his throne and slowly crept behind them. The guard must have noticed Brogue too because he turned quickly and stabbed the King in the gut. After that everything went in slow motion. Red got the guard down to the floor. I ran over to the King. He was bleeding badly.

"The King needs to go to the infirmary and fast! Go put that guard in the hole with the others," I shouted to Ben. I lifted the King up by his arms and Red picked up his legs, while Ben took the guard outside.

We left the King in the care of the witches so that they could heal him. In the courtyard, the guards were coming out of the hole. I spotted Jani slowly backing his way out of the crowd, so I summoned the wind power and flung him back into the hole.

"No, he stays in there," I said, walking up to the hole and looking down at him. "You, my creepy little friend, can stay in there until you've thought long and hard about what you've done."

I looked over at Star, or should I say Hellsolo Eden, as her eyes are still silver. She looked so drained. I walked over to her and said, "Eden, you look tired. Do you want to go and rest a while?"

"No Felix, I will be fine."

I nodded at her and walked up a few of the steps so I could see everyone. "Can I have your attention? HEY!" I shouted. Everyone turned to me. It made me have a mini freak out inside. I know I wanted all their attention, but jeez. "I have a little bit of bad news. King Brogue was stabbed. He's in the infirmary now, it looks like he will be ok, but until then I will be his stand-in." There were murmurs throughout the crowd and a lot of confused looks. Granddad Felix quickly came up the steps and whispered in my ear, "Felix, we need to talk. You can't just announce that you are King."

"Come with me," I said, turning away from him.

He didn't talk to me until we were in the throne room. "Felix, what the hell are you doing?" my Granddad asked.

I sat down on the throne with a bump, put my head in my hands and lent back. I didn't like the feeling that I got sitting on the throne.

I didn't notice that my Granddad had moved to my side. He put his hand on the top of my head and said, "Felix, what is going on? You know you can tell me what is bothering you."

I took a deep breath and moved my hands away from my head, looking up at my Granddad's concerned face. Do I tell him that I've been foreseen as the true King or not? "Granddad, I'm…" I began.

Then the doors flew open and Bruno, the young guard, came in and said, "Sorry sir, but the infirmary needs you, it's urgent."

I nodded at Bruno, looked at my Granddad and said, "We will talk about this later."

I left him in the throne room as I went with Bruno. "I never said thank you for not killing me, after I nearly killed you," he said sheepishly.

"That's ok. You were under a spell. You didn't really know what you were doing. Just forget it."

"Ok, thanks anyway."

I ruffled his hair and laughed.

In the infirmary, one of the witches told me that they needed my help. More precisely, they needed my energy power because King Brogue had lost a lot of blood. He needed an energy boost. I could feel his energy was very weak, so I sat there with him; my hand on his for a few hours, slowly building his energy up so it didn't overwhelm him.

I was shattered when I left to go back to the throne room. No one was there, so I sat back down on the throne. I was exhausted. I tucked my feet up and fell asleep on the throne; it was not comfortable at all, but I didn't care.

In the morning I woke up with Red in my face.

"Oh god. Why the hell you looking at me like that?" I asked, sitting up and rubbing my eyes.

"We've been waiting for ages for you to wake up. We need to go home. Mum and Dad will be worried that we aren't there."

Ohno. Everyone that's here with me is dead in the real world. I had to send them back, but I couldn't leave here because I'd said I was going to look after the Kingdom. "I will have to do it quickly, but I can't leave here for too long."

CHAPTER FOURTEEN

I went back to the real world and pulled everyone back through the portal with me.

Star didn't want to leave me in Alicade, but I didn't want her away from her family. They needed her. They all went back to their bodies when I pulled them back to reality.

Kava stayed back in Alicade while I was in our world. It was still night here, so I told Red and Ben to tell our parents about what had happened; and that I AM NOT DEAD! I asked them to let Mum and Dad know that I will be staying in Alicade for a while, just until things get sorted out. I also told them to find Kava's body and put it in a safe place, so Freddy wouldn't see it.

"Please don't let Freddy come in here and see me like this," I said to them.

"We won't bro," they replied in unison.

When Ben and Red left my room, I locked the door and lay on my bed. I was just about to go back to Alicade when I heard a voice in the dark.

"Please don't leave me here," it said – it was Star. She sounded upset. I sat up on my bed as she sat next to me.

"I have to, I'm acting King."

"Can't your granddad do it? Please stay…or you can take me back with you?"

"Star, it's too dangerous."

"Don't give me that, Felix. You pulled me through to fight with you. Don't you think *that* was dangerous?" She was right. "Please Felix," Star pleaded.

"Ok, but you need to go tell your family that you're coming with me. There is no way in *hell* I'm going to tell them."

"I will. I'll go now. Please don't leave without me."

"I would never do that," I promised.

Star gave me a quick kiss and she was gone. I suppose I could go get something to eat while I waited. I hadn't eaten since before the battle in Alicade and I was starving.

I was sat at the table eating some cereal when Star walked into the kitchen and said, "You ready?"

I had a mouthful of cereal and nodded. We went back to my room and I locked the door again. "So…how did your family take it? Do they want to kill me?" I said, as I lay back down on my bed. Before I could grab Balthazar's journal, Star got on the bed too. "No, they don't, but they are *not* happy. I told them I will be gone for a few days."

"I can cope with them not liking me for a while," I said, not all that surprised that Calvin and Chadwick had taken the news that Star wanted to come back to Alicade with me badly.

"What's that?" Star asked.

"It's Balthazar's journal," I said, as I held the book close.

I closed my eyes and thought about the big, dark green throne. My head started to spin and before I knew it, I was in the throne room, where Kava and Bruno were stood in front of the throne. I pulled Star back through the portal with me.

"Where's my Granddad?" I asked.

"He's in the infirmary with the King," said Kava, shaking my hand.

"Ok, thanks. Star, please stay here with Kava and Bruno."

"Why can't I come with you?" Star asked as she held my hand.

"I need to talk to my Granddad alone for a bit. Kava can show you to your room. Star, I'll come and find you later and we can talk," I said, as I kissed her cheek and left the room.

In the infirmary, my Grandad was stood at the end of King Brogue's bed. The king was still asleep. "How is he?" I enquired, standing next to my Granddad.

"He's a lot better. He has been awake. Why have you brought that book back here?"

"There's something I need to talk to you and the King about. It's about something that's written in here, but I don't know how to explain it without showing you."

"Felix, my boy, you know we cannot read that book."

God, he was right as well. How was I going to be able to show him what it said in the book?

"Felix Jr, is that you?" the Kind said groggily.

"Yes, it's me King Brogue."

"My King, Felix has something to tell us," said Granddad Felix.

"Well, erm, yes. I wanted to show you both something in this book, but I forgot that no one apart from me can read it," I explained.

"Felix Jr, I think I know what you are going to tell me," said King Brogue, as he struggled to sit up. I doubt it, I thought as I quickly moved over the King and helped him up, as did my Granddad on the King's other side. "The book told you that you were to be the true King."

"What?" Granddad Felix said, shocked.

"Yes, how did you know?" I said, grabbing the book off the table.

"I'm not just a King," Brogue explained. "I have the power of foresight. Not very many people know, and I rarely use it." The shocked expression on my Grandad's face told me that he wasn't in the know about Brogue's powers either. "I saw myself die and then you were crowned King."

"But you're not dead, so you can carry on being King," I said, in a little bit of a panic.

King Brogue laughed and said, "I'm getting really old now, my boy. I think it's time you stepped up and took responsibility."

"But I'm only 17. I can't be King, not yet. I can't just leave everyone on the other side and stay here full-time. I have family and friends out there that need me," I said. My chest felt like it was closing in on me, my breathing started to shorten. I was in full panic attack. The last thing I remember was my head hitting the side of the bed as I fainted.

I woke up in my room, with Star curled up beside me. I turned to the side, so I was facing her. I stroked her face. As I did, I noticed that the ends of her hair were red, so I pulled some of the energy out of her before she woke up.

I pulled her closer. Wrapping my arms around her, I fell quickly back to sleep.

In the morning, I hadn't realised that Star had gotten out of bed, so I woke up with Kava in my face. "What the hell, Kava? What are you doing?" Kava just laughed. "Are you trying to kill me?"

"Why would I want to kill the King?" he asked.

"What are you talking about, Kava?" I said, trying to play dumb about him calling me King, but Kava had always known when I was lying. I'm bad at it, apparently.

"I know everything. King Brogue, well it's just Brogue now, just renounced the crown and named you his successor. When were you going to tell me? We have been friends, a long time, Felix," Kava said, straightening up and crossing his arms over his chest.

"I wanted to tell you, but I didn't know how you were going to take it. When Chadwick confirmed it –"

"What, my brother knew?" Star interrupted from the other side of the room.

I looked over at her. She didn't look happy with me. "Well yeah. He found out when he told me about Karl. I didn't want anyone to know because I didn't know if I really wanted it or not."

Now it was Kava that wasn't happy. "Felix, being King is a great honour. You cannot pass this up," he said.

"Why can't I? It means I'll have to leave the real world to run this one. I can't just leave, Kava. My family are over there." I could feel my chest beginning to tighten. *Oh god, this can't be happening again,* I thought.

"Who said you have to stay this side?" Kava said. I looked at him, confused. "Felix, who said you have to stay in Alicade?" he repeated.

"No one, I just assumed I had to. King Brogue stays here."

"That's because he is dead in the real world. You, Felix, are not. You can come and go as you please. All you have to do is appoint someone to run Alicade while you are not here. Remember, the Glacier; Masguard; Camforge and Waterfall all have their own monarchy, so they have their own Kings and Queens. It's just that you are King over them all."

"So, when I become King, I can still go home?"

Kava just nodded. The relief flooded through my body and I lay back down on my bed and said, "I think I need a nap."

Kava laughed and said, "Get up, my King. We need to go."

"Please don't call me that," I said, rubbing my hands over my face to try and wake myself up.

"But it is your title now. You are King Felix of Alicade and the Arcana."

I got out of bed and said, "Arcana?"

"It's the collective name for all the five realms. It's what this reality is called," Kava explained.

"Ok. I need to get dressed. I'll meet you down in the kitchen," I said, as I put my hand on Kava's shoulder.

"You're in luck today, Felix. Trey is on kitchen duties." Kava said as he left.

"Oh YESSSSS, bacon and mushroom omelette," I said as I took my top off.

"I take it you like his omelette then?"

Star.

"Holy crap, I forgot you were here," I said, covering my bare chest with my top.

"It's nothing I've not seen before, Felix," Star laughed. I turned around, embarrassed. "Wow Felix! The symbol on your back has changed. It's complete. Wow, it looks amazing," Star said, touching it.

"With everything that's gone on, I'd completely forgotten about it. I'll talk to my Granddad about it later," I said, as I went into the bathroom to get showered and dressed.

Star and I walked hand-in-hand to the kitchen and there it was: my bacon and mushroom omelette. Let me tell you something, Trey was a wizard in the kitchen. He only works in here a few times a month, but when I was stuck here before, I was always first in line for his food.

I was quiet while I was eating my food. "I can't believe you're going to be King, it sounds so crazy," said Star.

"Star, if I was you, I wouldn't disturb him while he is eating Trey's cooking. It's not a pretty sight. He will get all shouty and then he whinges all day," said Kava, tucking into his own omelette. Star just laughed.

Later in the day, I left Star in the huge library. She was as amazed as I was when I first saw it. I went to the throne room through the secret door behind the throne.

King Brogue was sat on the throne, with my Granddad stood in front of him; and they were talking about some banquet for the ceremony.

"Felix," the King was saying to my Granddad, "Please arrange for Trey to do the food and ask John to decorate the hall for the feast. I want this to be perfect for Felix Jr"

"You know you don't need to do all this for me," I said. "I will just be happy with Trey cooking me some good food, in the company of some good friends."

"But you are King now, you deserve the best."

"I'm not King quite yet."

"But in a few short hours, you will be."

"Kava said that I don't have to stay on this side. He said that I can appoint someone to run Alicade while I'm not here. I've been thinking, Brogue: as you know everything already, would you like to be the one I appoint?"

King Brogue stood up and walked over to me. "That is right, you can appoint someone. But I don't think I'm the one that it should be."

"Then who? I don't know many people. The only ones I truly trust are you, Granddad and Kava."

"I think my time is up. It's time for a new generation to step up," King Brogue said, as he gestured for me to sit in the chair.

I shook my head no and said, "If not you, then who? Who do I choose?"

"How about Kava?" Granddad Felix said.

"I can't ask Kava to do it. I need him with me on the other side. I need all the support I can get with Annadora, but I could possibly ask him once it's done. I don't know if he wants to stay this side now, he's been out there."

"You can only but ask him. Ok, how about this? We can appoint one of the other Kings to sit here for the time being and Felix Senior and I will come to help you on the other side," said King Brogue.

I suppose I should stop calling him King now that he has renounced the throne to me. "Yes, that's a good idea, but who will do it? I've never met any of the other Kings," I asked.

"You will meet them tonight at the feast for the handover ceremony, but I think it should be King Alexander," King Brogue replied.

"King Alexander the Great?" I joked.

King Brogue looked at me, confused.

"Felix, this is not the time for jokes," my Granddad said, telling me off.

"Sorry." I turned to Brogue and said, "You won't have heard of him here. A lot of you are dead in the real world. My world had a great King once named Alexander. I was trying to be funny. Maybe our King Alexander could have been an avatar too. So, who is *your* King Alexander?"

"He is the King of the Glacier. But with the company that you keep, I'm not too sure that's a wise choice," Granddad Felix said, looking over to King Brogue; who rubbed his chin and sat back down on the throne, deep in thought.

"What do you mean by 'the company I keep?'" I asked, confused.

"Jr, it's the Redfield's. The King of the Glacier is King Alexander

Redfield. He's Chadwick and Star's Grandfather." I wasn't too

shocked, as I already knew that Star was a princess. "Felix, did

you know?" Granddad said, looking at me strangely.

"Did I know what? That Chadwick and Star were royalty? Yes, I

knew. Eden told me by mistake."

"Eden? Who is Eden?" Granddad asked.

"Eden is the Hellsolo that's inside Star," I said.

As soon as I'd said it, I thought my Granddad's eyes were going to

pop out of his head. He took a step towards me. "Felix, you never

told me she has a Hellsolo. This changes things."

"Jr, is Star here in Alicade?" Brogue said, standing up again.

"What the hell is going on?" I said. "I don't understand."

"Felix, Hellsolo's are beings of pure evil," Granddad said.

"But Eden isn't like that. Hellsolo Blood wolf on the other hand,

he is one scary person. He's the one in Calvin. I had to drain him

of powers once and, oh my god, the power knocked me out for

hours."

"You *defeated* a Hellsolo?" Brogue said, surprised.

"Yes, with Hellsolo Eden's help."

"So, is Miss Redfield here?" asked Brogue again.

"Yes, she's in the library."

"We shall go talk to her there then."

"No, I'll bring her here, to the throne room," I said. I was getting a strange vibe from them both.

I went back down the secret passageway to get Star. She had her head buried in a book about witches. "Hey Star," I said in greeting.

"Hi, Felix. This place is amazing!"

I smiled at her, as I know what it's like being in here for the first time. "Star, I need you to come with me to talk to the King and my Granddad."

"I thought you were King now?" she said, as she looked up from the book.

"Not until later. I'll be crowned at the feast. But I need you to be on your toes until then. I've got a horrible feeling that they're both up to something. I told them that you have a Hellsolo inside you and they freaked out."

"Why did they do that?" asked Star.

"He – my Granddad that is – said that all Hellsolo's are pure evil, but I tried to tell them that Eden was different. She's not evil," I said.

"What do you think they want with me?" Star said as we left the library. She sounded scared.

We went into the secret passage and walked back to the throne room. Come to think of it, I think we can stop calling the passageway a 'secret' now. I think half of Alicade knows it's here.

"Star, I need to tell you something before we get there. Erm well, the feast tonight and the handover ceremony, there's going to be lots of people there."

"What are you getting at, Felix? Are you going to ask me to be your date?"

I had to hide my smile, as I had assumed, we would be going together. "I thought we would be going together," I spoke my thought aloud.

"How do you know that someone hasn't already asked me?" Star joked.

"Who? You don't know anyone."

"I know Kava."

"Did Kava really ask you to go with him?" I said, as jealousy rushed through me. *How could one of my best friends ask Star out?* I could feel the fire flow through my veins. I felt betrayed. Star tapped me on the shoulder and started laughing. "If only you could see your face, Felix. I was only joking. Of course, I'll go with you."

"Please don't do that again. I wanted to kill him. I think it's time to detach my emotions from my powers again, so that I don't hurt anyone. But anyway, that wasn't what I wanted to talk to you about. I wanted to tell you that at this feast, your... erm..."

"Just spit it out, Felix," Star said.

"Your Grandfather will be there."

Star stopped in her tracks.

"I'm sorry," I went on. "I've only just found out. He's the King of the Glacier," I said, to fill the silence. Star just stared at me with a blank look on her face. "Star, please say something."

"What do you want me to say? You want me to say that I'm happy about it? No Felix, I'm not happy about it. He kicked my family out because my Dad fell in love with my Mum. Hang on, why is he here? He wasn't an avatar."

That's right, I thought. *Only avatars can come through the portal.* It just hit me. How did Kayos get through the portal? He wasn't an avatar either.

"Come on. We need to go and talk to them; and we will find out," I said, as I took Star's hand and went through the door to the back of the throne.

When we got into the throne room, King Brogue and my Granddad were still there, waiting for us. "Star, this is King Brogue and my Great Granddad Felix," I said, by way of introduction.

Star smiled and nodded.

"Miss. Redfield, it's a pleasure to meet you," King Brogue said, holding his hand out.

Star shook it; then she shook my Granddad's hand too. "So, you two have a problem with my Hellsolo?" Star asked, getting straight to the point.

"Well, Miss. Redfield, as you know, Hellsolo's can easily corrupt their hosts into doing bad things unless they are locked up," said Granddad Felix.

"Locked up?" I asked, confused.

"Yes, locked up inside their hosts, so that they can't come out."

"There's nothing wrong with my Hellsolo," Star said, crossing her arms over her chest.

"What about the time you went with your Mother? Your Hellsolo was present then, am I right? Didn't it nearly kill your brother Chadwick?"

"*Granddad*! I told you that in confidence," I said, not happy that he was interrogating Star like this.

"That was then, this is now. She's changed. She was the one who removed the dark mark from all your guards. If it wasn't for her, you would most probably still be in that gross dungeon," Star said, getting angry. She was right and I wasn't going to stop her from telling the truth. "If she's so bad, then why would she help us in your fight? Please explain."

"Ok, Miss. Redfield. We understand that you're upset, but we just need to make sure that you're not going to use your Hellsolo on us and massacre our people," Brogue said.

How could he say that? I thought. *Star would never do something like that.*

"In the nearly 10 years I've had Hellsolo Eden, I've only turned bad once. I was being coerced by my Mother then. I have nothing to do with her anymore. Now I'm with Felix, trying to catch her," Star explained.

I went to sit down on my soon to be throne. Who doesn't love a good argument? They stood there talking for a while. I won't bore you with the details, but essentially, they were worried that Star would turn as crazy as Hellsolo Eden.

"Jr, are we boring you?" Brogue said.

Crap, I must have nodded off. "No, no I'm good. What's up?" I said.

"Star wanted to know about how the portal works?" Granddad said.

"We both want to know about it," I said. "We wanted to know how King Alexander got to Alicade; and Kayos as well. They're not avatars, so how did they get through the portal?"

"Jr, Hellsolo's can travel through the portal too. It's not easy, but they can do it. Star's here isn't she?" Brogue said.

"Yes, she is Brogue, but she didn't travel here using her own power. I pulled her energy through the portal along with mine."

"Well, when King Alexander arrives later, you can ask him. I think it's time for me to rest."

"Ok my King, I will escort you back to your room," said Granddad Felix.

"Felix Senior, it won't be long until you have to call you're Great Grandson King."

My Granddad looked over at me with a huge, proud smile on his face. "Have a good rest. We will see you later. I'm going to show Star around a little before we go home tomorrow," I said.

"You're going back so soon. But you just got here," said Brogue. I looked at Star and she just nodded at me, answering my unasked question. "Ok, we will stay a few days, but we have to be back by Friday in the real world. Do you think you will still be up for coming with us?"

"We will be ready," Brogue said, and then he and Granddad Felix left.

"Well, that went well," I said.

Star came and sat next to me, on my throne; and put her head on my shoulder and replied: "Yes, it did."

CHAPTER FIFTEEN

I took Star on a tour of Alicade and showed her part of the wall of water that surrounds the Kingdom. Kava came along too, as did Bruno. Kava seems to have taken him under his wing, just like he did with me when I got here.

We were all sat up on the hill, overlooking the city, when people started turning up in their fancy carriages. Kava was telling us who they were and where they were from. We couldn't see their faces, but Kava could tell by the different carriages where they had come from.

After a while, Kava and Bruno started play fighting. I say play fighting: it was Kava's way of seeing how good a fighter Bruno was.

All of a sudden there was a loud fanfare of music and a huge white carriage, drawn by two rows of three white horses, approached us. It was stunning to look at. "Hey, Kava? Who's that?" I shouted.

"*That,* my King, is the King of the Glacier," he replied.

I turned to look at Star. "That's him, isn't it?" she said, she hadn't heard Kava over all the noise.

"Yeah, it is."

Kava looked at us, confused; and said, "Am I missing something?"

"Doesn't Kava know?" Star asked me.

"No, I didn't tell anyone else. It's not my secret to tell. I only spoke to my Granddad and the King because I had to."

"The *old* King," Kava interrupted.

"I'm not King yet. Not until the handover ceremony. I'm more like 'King-To-Be'."

Star cut in. "Kava, I'm the Granddaughter of King Alexander." Kava and Bruno fell silent as we watched the carriage go through the wall of water. "I didn't even twig that your surnames were the same," Kava said, adding hastily, "Your Highness."

Star looked as uncomfortable with her proper title as I was with my new one. Kava always was a stickler for tradition. "Come on," I said. "I think it's time we should be getting back. I don't think people will be happy if they have turned up to meet me and I'm not there."

We all raced down the hill. I think Kava cheated; he beat us all. I, obviously, fell over and landed in a huge puddle of mud. I was literally coated in mud. We tried to sneak past the people in the throne room, but my Granddad spotted me.

"Felix my boy, come here."

I popped my head around the door. In the throne room, there were about ten people, all looking at me. "Can you give me fifteen minutes? I'm a little dirty."

I could hear Kava and Bruno laugh. I kicked my foot out and it caught Bruno on the back of the leg. He fell to the ground, which only made Kava laugh louder.

"Ok, but please hurry. Everyone is very eager to meet you."

I smiled and nodded. I noticed one person who stood out from the others. He hadn't turned my way, so I glanced at him again quickly, before we ran down the hall – well, Bruno limped a little. Star went to her room. I had sent for someone to get some clothes for her. I jumped into the shower and got all the mud off, got dressed in some smart clothes. I'm meeting – and *becoming* – royalty, I might as well look nice. I still had my clothes from when I was stuck here all those Alicade years ago.

Kava and Bruno knocked at the door. "Come in, I'm nearly ready," I shouted out; and they came strolling in.

"Felix, what are you wearing?" Kava asked, looking at me strangely.

I looked at myself in the mirror. "Black trousers and a white shirt. What's wrong with that? I'm not going to do down there naked, am I?" I laughed.

"It looks fine, but why are you not wearing your armour?" Kava asked.

We all looked at my armour, standing there in the corner of my room. "But it's a bit battered. I should have gotten a new set."

"No, my King, this one is better. It shows that you are a warrior. It shows that you will fight for your people if need be," said Bruno, getting excited.

I looked over at my suit of armour again. "Bruno, please escort Star to the throne room; and I will help the King get ready." Kava smiled at me.

Bruno rushed out of the room. At that moment, it kind of hit me that this was really happening. I was going to be the King of Alicade and the Arcana. "Kava, I want you to be my number two. If I'm not here, then you're in charge."

"But I thought King Alexander was going to be your second in command?"

"Yes, he is for now, at least until Annadora is caught and in the dungeon of Falkor. After we've completed our mission though, I want it to be you. Please say you'll do it."

"But that would mean that I couldn't leave Alicade anymore as one of us would have to be here at all times and I cannot go to the other side without your help."

Kava looked sad, as I knew he would.

He helped me put my chest and back guards on. Then I tied the left side of my armour up, while he tightened the right side. I'd forgotten how tight this thing was. I put my hand on his shoulder and said, "It's ok if you don't want to be my number two."

"It's not that. It's just that I've been out there now, and the thought of not being able to go back…" he trailed off.

"Not a word more. I'll find someone else to do it. You are my friend, so I don't want you to do something that you don't want to. Where is my sword?"

Kava turned and picked it up off the bed, handing it to me. I tied the belt around my waist and pulled my sword from its sheath.

"Hello beautiful, missed me?" I said, examining the sword's fine blade all the way down to the guard and hilt.

"Felix, it's still weird that you talk to your sword," Kava said.

"Shush. Don't listen to him, he doesn't know what he's saying."

Kava rolled his eyes and asked, "Do you want me to leave you two alone for a while?"

I put my sword back in its sheath and said, "Come on, let's go and make me a King."

We both left for the throne room.

I was so nervous that I had to stop a few times to catch my breath on the way there. I was getting more and more nervous the closer we got.

We stood outside the throne room and we could hear people talking. I took a deep breath and walked in with him close behind.

"Jr, over here," Brogue called me over.

I noticed Star standing over with Bruno. "Go see if she's ok," I said to Kava.

"Ok, my King," he replied, as he started off towards Star.

I went and stood with Brogue. "King Brogue," I addressed him. Even though I'd stopped thinking of him as the King, I thought it best to use his title in public. I hadn't been officially crowned yet, after all.

"Looking good Felix," he said. "That armour still looks impressive on you."

"Thanks, I thought it would be a bit tight."

"Jr, this is King Alexander, he will be looking after things while you're away."

"Hello, King Alexander, nice to meet you," I said.

"Likewise, Felix," said King Alexander. "I hear you are friends with my Grandchildren?"

"Yes, I am. Star is here, do you want to meet her?"

As soon as I said it, I regretted it, as I'd never actually asked Star if *she* wanted to meet *him*. "Not right now," he replied.

"I think we should get the handing over ceremony started?" said Brogue. I nodded and followed him to the throne. "Can I have everyone's attention please?" Everyone turned to look at us. I was freaking out inside but looking over to my friends calmed me down a bit. "I would like to introduce you all to Felix Moon Jr, the great Grandson to our very own Felix Moon Senior. He has been named as my successor."

There were murmurs around the room at this, but Brogue ignored them and continued, "I have brought you all here to bear witness to the handing over of the crown."

Crown, I thought. I looked up at him and there it was. How have I never noticed it before? He must have never worn it in front of me before. It was silver and the King had jet back hair, so I would have noticed it if he had. It also had red, green, blue and white gems dotted around it. It was impressive.

I looked back around the room and I noticed that there were a few other people that had their own crowns on their heads. However, none of those crowns were as ornate as Brogue's – or should I say mine, now?

"Jr please, sit down on the throne," Brogue ordered.

I looked at him and nodded.

As I sat down, all eyes were on me. Crap, I just thought, do I have to give a speech? I hoped not. King Brogue took the crown off his head and said, "With the power vested in me as the King of Alicade and the Arcana, I pronounce *you*, Felix Moon, my successor!"

He slowly placed the crown on my head. *'Wow that's heavy, no wonder he doesn't wear it often,* I thought.

Everyone started clapping. I could feel the tears welling up inside me, but I didn't let them fall. I couldn't let them fall. I am King now; and it wouldn't look good to my people if the first thing I did as their new ruler was cry my eyes out.

I sat there, not knowing what to do. "Jr, do you want to say a few words?" Brogue said.

I looked up at him and replied, "Erm yes, thanks…I mean, thank you, King Brogue. I'm very honoured. Thank you to everyone who has come to witness the handover. I would like to thank my friends and family here; and those in the other world, for all their support. I don't think I could've done this without you all, thanks."

Everyone started clapping. "Well done, Jr. Come on, let me introduce you to some of the other Kings and Queens of the Arcana."

"Ok, King Brogue."

"Jr, you are the King now. I am just plain old Brogue."

Wow, that's right. It didn't feel right, just calling him Brogue. I know I'd joked around before, but that was just to piss Jani off. And it was one think not to think of him as a King, but quite another to say it out loud.

We walked around the room, meeting lots of people as we went. We met King Yuri and Queen Alaska, from Masguard; King Tobias and Queen Misha, from Camforge and King Quinton and Queen Harper, form Wadefall. I had already met King Alexander, of course.

Walking over to my friends, I felt shattered; and I was starving.

"Felix, you look very good in your armour," Star said, with a smile on her face.

"Thanks. I can't wait to get it off, though. I had forgotten how heavy it is. At least I have my baby back!"

"Oh god, Felix, don't start," Kava said, putting a hand over his eyes.

Star and Bruno looked confused. I had to show them. I smiled as I pulled my sword out. "*This* is my baby," I announced.

Bruno burst out laughing, so I gave him an evil look. "I'm sorry my King," he said. "But you are so funny!"

"Do you want me to stab you? I can, I'm King now. Stop bloody laughing, everyone is looking now."

"Ok my King, I'm sorry," Bruno said, trying to stop laughing.

"I can't believe your laughing at my baby," I said, disappointed in Bruno.

"Stop calling it your baby then," Star said, trying not to laugh too.

I put my sword back in its sheath. "I'm disappointed in you all. I'm upset now," I said, pulling a sad face.

"Oh Felix, don't cry, it's a… lovely sword," Star said, putting her arms around my neck and giving me a little kiss.

"King Felix, this is not an appropriate time for that," Kava said.

I looked over at him. "What? It was only a little kiss!"

Kava nodded over to where everyone was stood looking at us. Star quickly let go and turned around. "Show's over," I said, turning around too.

"My King, you are as red as the roses," Bruno whispered.

I rolled my eyes. I knew very well how red I was. I could feel my cheeks burning. Star started to laugh, so I did as well.

"Everyone, the banquet is ready," said Trey, who was stood at the door.

Let's just say I was the first one out of the door. I love Star, my friends and family, but I think I love Trey's food more.

I ate well that night, maybe a little too well. Ok, ok, I ate way too much and now I'm hurting, you happy? This armour has no give in it whatsoever; and with all the food I had eaten, I really needed to take it off. So, I excused myself from the table.

When I was in my room, struggling to take my armour off, there was a knock at the door. "Come in," I called out.

Star walked in and said, "I thought you might need some help."

"Oh my god, yes. I just can't reach to get this chest plate off."

"You probably should've stopped at your fourth helping of the chocolate cake," Star laughed.

"But it was sooo good!"

"I know it was. Turn around."

Star undid the straps. "Oh yes, that feels so much better, my belly has room to stretch."

Star hugged me from behind. "Thanks for letting me come back with you. I'm glad I was one of the witnesses to your coronation."

I turned in her arms, so we were facing each other. "I wouldn't want it any other way. If I'm the King, does that make you my Queen?"

Star smiled and put her head on my chest. I took off my crown and put it on her head. She looked up at me. "Will you be my Queen?"

"Felix, are you asking me to marry you? Don't you think we are too young to be married?"

"Ok, I think that came out wrong. I was asking if you would like to be my girlfriend? You know, officially?"

I could see the weight visibly lift off her shoulders when she realised what I was asking. "Oh right. But that won't make me a Queen," she laughed.

"But it will make you *my* Queen," I said as I lent down and gave her a gentle kiss.

"Ok, it's official, I'll be your girlfriend," she replied.

I hugged her tight and said, "We'd better be getting back. The King shouldn't be missing for too long at his own party." My heart was racing I was so happy.

"Come on my King, let's go," Star said, putting the crown back on my head.

Walking back into the dining hall I could smell Trey's food and I headed towards the food table, but Star pulled me away. It was probably for the best, I was still hurting a little. It was strange to hear people greeting me as the King at first. I kept looking behind me for King Brogue. *Just Brogue now,* I reminded myself.

We sat back at our table and we all talked and joked around, until King Alexander stood in front of our table. "My King, may I have a word?" he asked.

"You may," I said, still sitting down.

"Privately, I think he means," Kava said, nudging me.

"Oh yes, sorry. I will meet you in the throne room in a minute."

"Thank you, my King," King Alexander said, bowing his head and walking off.

"What do you think *he* wants?" asked Star, looking nervous.

"I don't know, but I'll soon find out," I said, getting up and walking to my throne room.

King Alexander as stood next to the throne, waiting. I sat down on the throne. Nope, I still didn't like the feeling, so I stood up.

"King Alexander, you wanted a word? How can I help you?"

"I just need to know some details about me being your stand in?"

"And you couldn't ask me about this at the table?" I replied, confused.

King Alexander was starting to look uncomfortable. "This is not about you standing in for me, is it? It's about Star?"

King Alexander stopped fidgeting. "I want to know your intentions for my Granddaughter?"

"And that's your business now?" Star said from behind me, making me jump.

"Princess Morningstar," King Alexander said, bowing his head. Star and I looked at each other. "Princess Morningstar?" I said.

"Yes, that's her official title," replied King Alexander.

"But you stripped my Father of his title?" said Star.

"Yes, that's true, but that doesn't apply to his children. So, you, Kayos and Chadwick are still Princes and a Princess."

I was still a little confused, so I said, "But you called her Princess Morningstar, why?"

"Morningstar is her name," he laughed and looked at us like we are crazy.

"My name isn't *Morningstar*, it's just start."

"I think that's a conversation you need to have with your Father," King Alexander said, still a little uncomfortable.

"Why won't you tell me? You're my Grandfather, after all," Star said.

"Because, I don't know why your Father chooses not to call you by your full name," Kind Alexander responded. "I got a letter saying that Prince Calvin had three children called Prince Kayos, Prince Chadwick and Princess Morningstar."

I could see tears running down Star's cheeks. I put my arm around her, King Alexander didn't like it too much, but I didn't really care.

"What does Morningstar mean?" I asked, but I never got a reply.

"King Alexander, your King asked you a question," I said in a raised voice. I didn't like the 'your King' quote, but it got through to him.

"Sorry," he said. "what star comes out in the morning, your Majesty? The sun, of course. Morningstar, how do you charge, your powers?"

"By the setting sun," Star replied.

"Have you ever tried the rising sun?"

"No, Mum said that it was only the setting sun that I get power from," Star said. She had stopped crying; she was more interested in what he had to say.

I let them talk for a while, my head started to drift off, and it got me to thinking. Star's real name is Morningstar, which means 'the sun'; and my surname is Moon, which obviously means 'the moon'. We are 'the sun and the moon'.,

"Holy crap," I said it a bit too loud, making Star jump a little.

"Felix, are you ok?" Star asked, putting a hand on my arm.

"Morningstar, he is the King, you have to address him as such," King Alexander admonished her.

"If she has to address me as King, then you have to address her as Princess, as that is *her* title," I ordered.

"As my King wishes. I'm sorry Princess Morningstar, my apologies," King Alexander said, bowing his head.

I turned around and said, "Star, help me lift up my top."

"*What?*" Star said surprised.

"Not like that. I want to show him the tattoo on my back." She laughed nervously but helped me pull it up. "King Alexander, do you know what this is?"

"Yes, my King, that is the mark of the mod avatar. Hang on, the bit in the middle is not. I've not seen it before."

"It's the sun and the moon," I said, looking over at Star; who was looking at me confused. "Think about it, you are Morningstar, 'the sun' and I'm Felix Moon, 'the moon'. It's about us."

I let my top just fall back down. I didn't tuck it back in. I can be a scruffy King if I want to. "It must be your destiny," said King Alexander.

I turned back around and said, "I remember talking to my Granddad and he said that she could be 'the one'. I'm drawn to Star, but it's strange as I have the same kind of pull towards my little brother Freddy. I love Freddy, but obviously, I'm not *in love* with him." As soon as I'd said the words, I instantly froze. Did I just say I was in love with Star without realising it?

I could see Star out the corner of my eye. She had a huge smile on her face. King Alexander, on the other hand, he looked pissed that I'd virtually declared my love for Star. I think we started a starring competition.

"Come on my King, we should be getting back to the dining hall. You have lots more people to meet," Star said.

I looked away from King Alexander first. I didn't like Star saying 'my King', but I should get used to it as it was my title now. She shouldn't have to call me that though. "Ok Princess Morningstar lead the way. Good evening, King Alexander," I said, nodding my head in his direction before following Star out the throne room.

Once out the room, Star stopped, turned and kissed me. "What was that for?" I asked, surprised.

"Just for being you, come on," she said.

Back in the dining room, we went to sit down next to our friends and the rest of the evening went fine. Some of the other Kings and Queens requested a meeting with me as well, but they just wanted to congratulate me. I asked them a few questions about their lives and about where they were from. I told them that once my mission in the real world was complete, I would make a visit to each realm.

The night finally drew to a close. I was shattered. Kava and Bruno weren't though, so they went to one of the training rooms to spar. I escorted Star back to her room and we stood there talking for a while. I couldn't help but yawn a few times.

"Am I boring you?" Star joked.

"You could never bore me. It's just been a long day."

"Ok, my King. You go and sleep if you want."

I put my head down and said, "Please don't call me that."

"But my Granddad was right. You are the King now and I should address you by your proper title."

"Please don't."

"Ok. Let's make a deal. I will only call you King when there are people around?" Star said, cupping my face in her hands.

"Ok," I said, as I leant forward and gave her gentle kiss.

"I will see you in the morning," Star said, as she went into her room.

"Night."

The walk back to my room wasn't that long, but it still gave me time to think. If the tattoo on my back was the mark of the mod avatar and the middle bit could be about Star and I, then I wondered what was in the middle of Baltazar's mark?

I got to my room and all I wanted to do was sleep, but I'd forgotten that I'd left my armour on my bed. I put it back on its stand and I lay down on my bed. My crown fell to the floor. To be honest, I had forgotten that it was on my head, which was surprising as it wasn't light. I picked it up and looked at it closely, it was really beautiful.

Everyone in the real world isn't going to believe me when I tell them that I'm now a King, I thought. *I am King Felix of Alicade and the Arcana,* I laughed to myself.

I put the crown on the table by my bed and soon fell asleep.

CHAPTER SIXTEEN

The next few weeks in Alicade were comprised of nothing but work for me. I had to have a good few meetings with people to let them know that King Alexander would be overseeing things while I was away. I put Bruno in temporary second in command; he wanted to come and fight with us, but I needed at least one person left behind in Alicade that I could completely trust.

Our last day in Alicade had finally arrived, and we were now due to go back to the real world. Everyone was gathered in the throne room. King Alexander was sat on my throne. I know I didn't like sitting on it, but I *definitely* didn't like anyone else sitting on it. Bruno was stood at King Alexander's side. He was dressed in his own suit of armour. It's a shame that I wasn't taking him with us because he was getting to be a good fighter, but like I said, I needed someone here I can trust. And finally, Granddad and Brogue were stood on the other side of the throne, talking.

Star and Kava walked up to me and she said, "So, are you ready to go home, my King?"

"I've told you not to call me that."

"Come on, everyone's ready." Star said, as she grabbed hold of my hand and pulled me over to where everyone else was standing.

I cleared my throat, and everyone turned to look at me. "Ok, this is how it's going to work. I'm going over first and take Star and Kava with me. I think I need to prepare my family for Granddad Felix arrival. They should be fine, but just to be on the safe side. Mum threw lots of stuff at me when I just walked in, back from the dead."

I laughed.

"That sounds like a good plan, my King," said Granddad Felix, putting his hand on my shoulder.

I nodded and sat down on the floor. I held Balthazar's journal in my right hand and my crown in my left. I thought about my bedroom and my soft, soft bed that I've missed so much. It didn't take long before the room started spinning. I closed my eyes in Alicade and opened them in the real world.

I was back! back in my room, in my bed. Star was next to me and she was dead...for the moment. She wasn't really dead. Well, yes, she *was* dead, but not for long. I'm not really getting any better at explaining how this portal thing works, am I?

I pulled her energy through the portal first. She inhaled a deep breath and started coughing. I held her close until she started breathing normally again. "You ok?" I asked, kissing her forehead.

"Yes, I'm fine. I really don't like that bit, it feels so wrong," she joked.

I'd pulled Kava through the portal too, but I didn't know where his body was when he dropped back into reality. I'd asked the Satan twins to move him somewhere safe before we'd left.

It was light outside when we started walking down the stairs. Kava made us jump when he came out of the twin's room. "They stuffed me in the bloody wardrobe," Kava said indignantly, rubbing his head. I couldn't help but laugh at him.

We walked into the kitchen.

Mum was cooking breakfast and Freddy was sat at his little blue table. "Fix, Fix, Fix is home," Freddy said, bouncing over to me.

I picked him up and said, "Hey, Mini-Me. Yes, I'm home now. Have you been good while I've been away?"

"Yep. Fix come play with me? You can be Thor," Freddy said, giving me his Thor figure.

"Not right now, buddy. I need to talk to Mummy and Daddy for a minute. Maybe later, ok."

"Ok, me hun-gy."

I put Freddy down and gave him his Thor toy back and he ran back to his table.

"Nice to have you back Felix, Star, Kava, you hungry?" Mum asked.

Kava sat down in a flash. "Yes, I'm starving Mrs. Moon."

"Mum, where's Dad?" I asked. "I need to talk to you both."

"He's at the same place he is every Thursday, he's at the shop," she replied.

I looked over at Star and said, "Please can you go and grab him for me?"

She nodded and in the blink of an eye, she was gone.

"Is everything ok, Felix?"

"Yes, everything's fine. I just need to talk to you both before I do something."

"Oh ok, sweetie," Mum said, before she went back to cooking breakfast.

It didn't take Star long to get back with my Dad. We all sat at the table and I explained what was about to happen. I told Mum and Dad that I was going to bring Granddad Felix through the portal. My Dad was really excited, as he hasn't seen him in 10 or so years. "Ok, one other thing. Erm, you're going hear them call me King Felix, I said."

"King?" they both said.

"Yes well...I went to Alicade a few days ago; and then got crowned King of Alicade and the Arcana," I said, as if it was the most normal thing in the world.

"What's the Arcana?" asked Mum.

"It's the name for all the places in the avatar world. There're five realms in all the Glacier; Masguard; Camforge; Wadefall and my

Kingdom, Alicade. The Arcana is the name given to all five. I now rule over all five."

Then, all of a sudden, my crown – that I know full well I'd left on my bed – was now sitting in the middle of the table. I looked over to Star and half smiled.

"Wow Felix is this your crown?" my Dad said, awed.

"Yes, yes, it is," I said simply.

My parents looked so proud of me and what I have achieved. Dad reached out to touch the crown, but stopped just short of it, then said, "You didn't have to kill the old King to get the throne, did you?"

"No Dad. I didn't, he's actually coming here with Granddad Felix. He renounced the throne and gave his crown to me. I'm the mod avatar, which makes me the one true King of Alicade and the Arcana."

Mum was crying.

"Fix, what's that?" Freddy asked, pointing to the crown.

"It's my crown, do you like it?" I asked.

"It's pretty," he replied.

I picked Freddy up and put him on my lap. "Do you want to try it on?"

"Yeah, yeah, yeah," he squealed in delight.

I placed it on his head and said, "I, King Felix, name you, Freddy Moon, Prince Freddy of Alicade and the Arcana."

The crown didn't fit him at all, but he loved it. It made me smile that he was so happy.

"King Fix, wow, just wow," Freddy beamed.

"My King, you do know that you really did just make young Freddy a Prince. I'm from Alicade, so I'm your witness," Kava said.

I looked over at Kava, shocked.

"You're joking?" Star said, before I could.

"Nope, you only need one witness to confirm the bestowing of a title; and I have no objections."

I didn't know what to say. I was still in a little bit of shock, so I settled for saying, "Erm well, next time stop me if I'm going to do something stupid." A horrible thought struck me. "Does that mean when I die, Freddy becomes King?"

"Yes, my King. That's what normally happens, unless you and Star have children" Kava laughed.

I completely ignored the bit about children, "How? Freddy isn't an avatar; how would he get to Alicade?" I said.

We all just looked at Kava, who'd stopped laughing. He didn't have an answer. Thankfully, just then, someone knocked at the door, breaking all our concentration. "I'll get it," Sue said, getting up.

"Hey Mrs. Moon," we heard from the front door. "Has Felix woken up yet?"

"Yes Sean, he's in the kitchen," came my Mum's reply.

I put Freddy down on my chair and got up to give Sean a hug. In the real world it's only been a few days, but in Alicade it's been weeks. "How's everything going?" I asked him.

"Ok, I guess. I'm just getting nervous about tomorrow," he replied.

I took in a deep breath and said, "Everything will be ok. Have you been training with your power?"

"Yes, Ben and Red have been taking me to Drake Forest to practice. Wow, Freddy, that's a wicked crown," Sean said, as we walked into the kitchen.

"Yeah, it's Fix crown," Freddy said happily.

Sean looked over at me and said, "Explain?"

"You are now looking at His Majesty, Felix Moon, the King of Alicade and the Arcana," I proclaimed, in an exaggerated tone. Sean's mouth popped open and I couldn't help but laugh. "Close your mouth, or you're going to catch flies. Freddy, do you want to show Sean my crown?"

"Yeah," Freddy said, jumping of the chair and running over to Sean. He held up his arms to be picked up and Sean did just that. Freddy took the crown off his own head and placed it on Sean's head instead, saying, "I call Sean King of the world!"

Star, my Mum, my Dad and I all looked over at Kava who was still eating. "You're fine," he chuckled between mouthfuls. "It's only the King's word that I can witness. Freddy is only a Prince, your safe."

"Prince? Have I missed something?" Sean asked, confused.

"I said something I shouldn't have without knowing what it would mean and now Freddy is the Prince of Alicade," I explained.

"Only you, Felix, would do something so bloody silly," Sean said, putting the crown on my head.

"I didn't really mean it! I was just messing around. How was I supposed to know?"

"To be fair, Felix, when you were crowned by the old King, Brogue; you had witnesses there too," Star said.

"Star, you are *not* making it better," I said playfully. "It was an accident, but if my little brother wanted to be a Prince, then he will be a Prince. Ok, I think it's time to bring over Granddad Felix and Brogue. I'll be back soon."

I sat on my bed crossed legged and closed my eyes to concentrate. I thought of my Granddad's energy first, he has an energy signature that you could never forget; it had such a deep hum.

It didn't take long to bring them both across. I was getting good at it now. "My King," they both said in unison.

"Ok we are in the real world now, so you don't have to call me King," I clarified; and prayed they wouldn't. My title had seemed fine in Alicade when I was in the palace or on my throne, but here, in my regular teenager's bedroom, it just felt stupid.

"But you are our King and we will address you appropriately," said Brogue.

I briefly wondered how it must feel for him, having been on the throne for so many years, to address someone else as King. "Ok, but I do have a little confession to make. I made Freddy a Prince by accident."

Brogue shook his head; and Granddad Felix just laughed.

I took them downstairs and into the kitchen where everyone was still sitting. Ben and Red had turned up and before I could interduce them, Ben shouted across the table, "Hey Felix, you going to make us Princes too?"

"No Ben, I'm not."

"That's not fair! You made Freddy a Prince," Red butted in.

"I didn't mean to do that. I gave you powers, what more do you bloody want?"

"We want to be Princes."

"Ok then, Red. I'll take your power away then you can be a Prince, deal?"

"Keep your titles," they both said together.

"That's what I thought," I said, laughing. "Mum, Dad, this is former King Brogue; and you know Great Granddad Felix, of course."

They all said hello. Mum and Dad both hugged Granddad Felix. Mum was definitely crying by this point.

My Dad was crying too, but he tried to hide it.

I went into the living room and most of the others followed me, just the adults stayed in the kitchen. We started to watch a movie. I had Star snuggled up on one side of me and Freddy on the other. I'd never felt happier than did in this exact moment. The two people I need the most are right here, next to me; and they are safe.

Freddy had fallen asleep watching the film; and we started talking about what we were going to do tomorrow. "So, who's had any ideas on what we are going to do?" asked Sean.

"I really don't know, Sean," I said. "I have nothing. It's so different fighting over in Alicade; I don't really know anyone over there. But here, it's a horrible feeling knowing that I'm fighting alongside friends and family. I just want to keep you all safe and out of the way, but I know I can't."

"It's ok Felix. We all know what we're getting ourselves into and we're with you 100%. We know you want to keep us safe, but you also know you can't do this by yourself," Red said, kneeling in front of me, as was Ben.

"King Felix, you'll have to start thinking like a King. You're going to have to start making decisions you're not going to like," Brogue said from behind me.

"Yes, I know that, but...we are in the real world, I'm not King here," I replied.

Brogue shook his head in disagreement. "Look around King Felix. There are three people from Alicade here and there are three avatars that you have made as well. They might not know it, but you are their King too. Then there's Prince Freddy, you have to show him how to be King someday."

"Freddy will never be King. I know I'll outlive everyone. I read in Baltazar's journal that when he hit 25 years old, he stopped ageing," I said, looking at everyone and getting upset with myself.

"Oh Felix, don't think like that," Star said, throwing her arms around me.

"Sorry," I said, hugging her tightly.

"How about this: we all go to Drake Forest early in the morning and plan where we will all stand?" she asked.

"Hang on, there's no water in Drake Forest," said Ben, looking over at me.

"You're right, there's not," I said. "Star can you bring Chadwick here; I need a word with him."

Star nodded. She disappeared and reappeared behind Red and Ben, who was still kneeling in front of me. She had brought a disgruntled looking Chadwick back with her.

"What the hell, Star? You could've let me get dressed first!" Chadwick said, standing there in only his trousers.

In a flash, Star threw a t-shirt at him, sat back down next to me and she said, "The King wants to ask you some questions."

I looked over at her reproachfully. She knows full well I don't like her calling me King. Chadwick put his top on and said, "King? What's going on?"

I looked back over at him and said, "I don't have time to explain, but you already knew I was going to be King. It just happened sooner than you foresaw. I need to know if the battle with Annadora happens at Drake Forest."

"I don't understand. That's where Annadora said it will be," Chadwick replied.

"Yes, well it has come to my attention that Drake Forest does not have a body of water to drown Karl in; and we know from your vision that he dies by drowning. I need you to use foresight to see if the battle really happens there. I need it doing now."

Chadwick looked around the room. "Ok, I'll be upstairs," he said, as he walked away.

"Star, why did you talk to him like that?" I whispered to her.

"Talk to him like what? You need answers and you need them now."

We just stared at each other. Why was she acting so strange?

"Star, can I have a private word with you?" I asked, getting up off the sofa gently so as not to wake Freddy up.

I walked through the kitchen and out the back door to the garden. I stood over by the pool, looking down at my reflection. The crown that Freddy had put back on my head was glistening in the water's reflection.

"What do you want to talk about?" Star questioned, walking up to me.

"I just want to know why you're acting so strange. You know I don't like it when you call me King."

"I know, but what Brogue said: that you are King to the others; he didn't include me in that. I just wanted you to know that you are my King too," she explained.

I put my arms around her and said, "I don't want you to call me that, please."

"Ok Felix, I won't. I'm sorry."

We kissed; it was a gentle kiss, but we were disturbed when Chadwick came out of the back door. "Put my sister down," Chadwick laughed, needless to say we stop kissing.

I gave Star a tight hug before letting her go. "So, what did you see?" I asked Chadwick.

"You were right. The battle with Annadora doesn't happen at Drake Forest. She lied to you. When you told me, it was at Drake Forest I didn't give it a second thought, but when I actually looked around, I didn't recognise the place."

"But was it still in a forest?"

"Yes," he said.

I rubbed my hands over my face, not knowing where else it could be. "Let's go in and ask the others. They might know where it could be."

We walked back into the house. Everyone was still in the living room, talking. I stood in front of everyone, trying to be Kingly (is that even a word? Probably not, but I'm going with it). I feel like a faker, but they all looked at me with bated breath.

"Ok, change of plan," I said.

"There was no plan to start with," Sean interrupted.

Red clipped Sean over the head and said, "Shush, peasant, the King is speaking."

I stared at Red in disbelief he'd just called me 'the King'. The twins and I had never had a good relationship before all this happened.

I remember one Halloween, when I was seven years old; they had scared me so much by jumping out at me or something falling on me. I was a nervous wreck, so jumpy that I'd had to have two weeks off school. If someone got to close too me, I would freak out and I would scream until they backed away from me. One day I just snapped out of it, but ever since then, I've called them the Satan Twins.

"King Felix, are you ok?" Brogue asked, bringing me back to reality.

I shook my head and said, "Erm yes, I'm fine. So, it's not happening at Drake Forest like Annadora said. I don't know of any other forest around here that has water in it."

"What about Lake Halo? It has forests with ponds scattered throughout," said Granddad Felix.

"That's right," I said. "There was a pond their near our log cabin."

"The one we nearly drowned you in," said Ben. I shot the twins an evil look. "Sorry," they said in unison, and hit each other around the head.

"But Lake Halo is close to 200miles away. Why would she go there?" Sean asked, confused.

I looked over at Granddad Felix and said, "That's where Baltazar is trapped, isn't it?"

"It is," he replied.

I rubbed my hands over my face. I was getting a bad feeling about this – well, a worse feeling than I'd already had, anyway.

"But my King, she cannot get to him. The crypt has the highest protection over it. There are also witches and avatars watching over it," explained my Granddad.

"But Granddad, you haven't been there in a loooong time. How do you know it's still protected?" I questioned and saw the colour drain out of his face.

"My King, I need to go back to Alicade, *quickly!*" Granddad Felix said.

"He cannot go, not this close to the battle. What if something happens and he cannot get back, or what if something happens this side; none of us can go back through the portal now," said Kava, standing up and squaring off in front of Granddad Felix.

I had forgotten he was here; he had been so quiet. I walked over to where Kava was standing, and I put my hand on his shoulder. I said, "It's ok, my friend, we will be quick. You are in charge while I'm gone. Come with me, Granddad."

I took him to my room. He lay on my bed and I sat in the chair. I let my head fill up with the image of the throne room and in no time, I was in my throne room. I startled King Alexander, who was reading a book on my throne. He quickly got up and said, "My King, back so soon?"

I walked over to my throne and sat down. I didn't like sitting on it, but I didn't like *him* sitting on it either. "I'm not staying. My Granddad needed to pop back for something."

"Oh right, where is he?"

"I've not pulled him back through the portal yet," I said, closing my eyes and pulling my Granddad's energy through. When I opened my eyes, he was stood in front of me. He nodded and scuttled out the doors.

"How's my Kingdom been since I've been gone? Nothing interesting has happened I presume, as you were sat here reading," I said.

"You have only been gone for a few days. The only news is that the man in the hole escaped," King Alexander explained.

"WHAT? HOW THE HELL DID THAT HAPPEN?" I shouted.

"I don't know."

"HOW DO YOU NOT KNOW?" I roared. I couldn't help but shout at him.

"I'm sorry my King," King Alexander said, shamefully bowing his head.

"I'd know that voice anywhere, King Felix," Bruno said, as rounded the corner. "Oh, not a happy King," he added, upon seeing my face.

"What's this, Bruno?" I asked, trying to calm my voice a little. "I here Jani has escaped. Wasn't anyone guarding him?"

"There was a guard stationed at the pit at all times, but after you left, the energy field around the hole got weaker and weaker; and he got out last night. I'm so sorry, my King," Bruno said, as he took to one knee in front of me in a low bow.

"You can stand Bruno. I just wish someone would have come and told me."

"But my King, you were in the real world. None of us knew where you were, and none of us would have been to your house in the real world. So even if we could get there, where would we have gone?"

"Good point, Bruno. Are you still alive in the real world?"

He just nodded.

"And you come from planet earth, right Bruno?" I asked.

King Alexander and Bruno both looked at me like I was off my meds and I was speaking in tongues. "Kava is from planet Nova. I didn't know there were other planets out there." Judging by the looks on their faces, they hadn't known of the existence of other planets either. I waved my hands, dismissing it. "Anyway, Bruno, I live at 24 Arch Close in Newport Falls. Star lives at number 23."

Bruno nodded and asked, "How long have you been here for? When are the others coming back? I want to show Kava my new moves."

I smiled at him. I remembered a time when I was excited to show Kava how well I was mastering my fighting skills as well. I replied "We're not finished over there, but soon we'll be back. A few weeks, maybe."

Bruno smiled at me, a smile that never touched his eyes. I knew that he was sad that all of his friends had up and left him; and he had to stay here and babysit King Alexander for me.

I'd asked Bruno before I left to keep a close eye on him. "King Alexander, who is out looking for Jani?" I addressed him.

"I've sent out Captain Javan and his men. The prisoner can only have a few hours on us, so Captain Javan assured me that he won't come back until Jani has been found," King Alexander replied and bowed his head.

I was so annoyed at him, more than I was with Bruno. King Alexander should've known better; he runs his own kingdom for Christ's sake. "I'm *not* best pleased about how my kingdom has been run in my absence. I've only been away for a few days and you have let a prisoner go free. Do you even know if he is in this world? Do you know if he is dead in the real world?" I said, getting angry.

"I'm sorry my King. I didn't think of that being a possibility."

"Is this how you run your own kingdom? King Alexander, if so, I think a new temporary King is needed."

"King Felix, he is doing his best," said Bruno, taking a step towards me.

I was slightly annoyed that Bruno was defending my stand-in. "Clearly his...*best*...is not good enough," I said, coldly. "He was sat here reading a book while Jani's out there somewhere. Have you all already forgotten that he overthrew Brogue in the few hours that our former King was at the Glacier? You know what? I can't deal with this right now. Bruno, please go and find my Granddad and tell him to hurry."

"Of course, my King," said Bruno, moving quickly out of the room. I rubbed my eyes and King Alexander, who was still stood there with his head bowed down to me, remained silent. What the hell was I going to do with him? "King Alexander, I had high hopes for you. I feel let down," I said, disappointed beyond measure.

"I'm sorry, my King. If this had happened in the Glacier, I would have been really angry."

"Then why didn't you get angry here? This is where I will be residing. I need people to know that they can trust the new King; and trust my judgment, but you are doing next to nothing to look for Jani. You only sent out Captain Javan and his men. You should have *everyone* out there looking for him!"

"I am *truly* sorry, King Felix. It will *never* happen again."

"It had better not. I will give you a second chance, don't screw it up," I warned.

"Thank you, my King. I won't."

I waved my hand at him and said, "You can go now."

King Alexander bowed his head and started walking out. I'd started feeling like I was being a little bit too harsh on him; he had sent people out looking for Mr. Creepy, after all. "King Alexander," I called after him. "Who is in the kitchen today? Do you want to talk properly, over some food?"

"That would be nice, my King. Erm, I'm not too sure who is in the kitchen today, but all I know, Bruno was laughing this morning about you not being here for the food."

I sat up straight on my throne. "Is Trey in the kitchen?" I asked. "Was he the one that cooked on the handover ceremony?"

"Yes."

"Then yes, it's him."

"I will meet you there" I said; then I legged it to the kitchen as fast as I could.

We stayed in Alicade for a few hours to have lunch (of course, Trey's cooking was outstanding). Granddad Felix had found what he was looking for. It was a book on all the avatars that where dead in the real world; and it turns out that Jani was still alive in the real world.

"Great! King Alexander, you might as well send for Captain Javan. Jani won't be anywhere in the Arcana. If I were him, I would have escaped to the real world like a shot," I said.

"Ok my King. I will send for him," King Alexander replied, as he bowed his head and left.

I looked over at Bruno, about to speak, but he cut across me and said, "You don't need to tell me that you're leaving again, I know."

"Before you know it, we will all be back," I said, trying to console him.

Bruno bowed his head too. "Ok my King. I hope to see you soon. I'd better go find King Alexander."

"Ok Bruno, see you soon," I replied, but he had already left the room.

Granddad Felix put his hand on my shoulder and said, "He will be fine. He knows you have an important job to do in the real world."

"I know. Are you ready to go?" I asked him.

"Yes, my King."

I took the book off him, as I didn't know if he could hold the book and bring it through the portal with him.

CHAPTER SEVENTEEN

n no time at all, I woke up in my room, as did Granddad Felix. I gave him back his book and we went downstairs.

While we were gone, Star's Dad, Calvin had turned up. I think this is the first time I've seen him since the protection spell with Hellsolo Blood wolf. I couldn't help but keep glancing over at him, just to make sure his eyes were still blue.

"It's ok Felix, Hellsolo Blood wolf will not come out," said Calvin not even looking at me.

I shivered, it was like he'd read my mind or something...could he even do that? I thought it best not to ask, so I just looked away from him. "Ok," I said, "When do we leave to go to Lake Halo?"

"It's a good few hours' drive," said Red.

"Star, couldn't you just teleport us there?" I asked her.

"Sorry, not this time. I can only teleport to places I've already been in person. I've never been to Lake Halo, so we'll have to do it the old-fashioned way," Star said, and gave me a quick kiss on the lips.

I froze. I could feel Calvin's eyes burning into me. I tried to ignore him, counting how many of us were going to Lake Halo in my head. There would be ten of us in total: Star; Sean; Kava; Red;

Ben; Chadwick; Calvin; Brogue; Granddad Felix and I. "Ok so there are 10 of us. We will need at least two cars," I said.

"How about you and Star go first then she could just come for us," Sean said, trying to hide a smile; his reaction to Calvin seeing mine and Star's kiss.

He is definitely going to get his butt kicked, I thought.

"Yes, that sounds like a good plan. Then we won't all be stuck in a car for hours," said Ben.

"I could go with that," Star said, as she put her arm around my waist. Oh my god, Calvin is actually going to kill me.

"My King, you haven't said anything, you ok?" said Kava, looking worried.

"Yes, I'm fine. That sounds good to me. Dad, can I borrow the car? But hang on a sec, neither of us can drive."

"I can. I learned while you were stuck in Alicade," Star said.

"Of course, son; I'll get you the car keys, along with the keys to the cabin."

Everything was starting to sound so wrong. It sounded like Star and I was going on a romantic holiday to the cabin. I felt like I wanted the floor to open up and swallow me whole. "Everyone, go and pack an overnight bag. We'll be staying there the night or two, so we will need to scout out the place," I said.

Kava, Brogue, Granddad Felix and Mum went back into the kitchen. Kava was still hungry, so Mum said she would make him a quick something before we were due to leave. Red and Ben

went to their room to pack and Star took Chadwick home. Calvin

said he wanted a word with me.

Let's just say I was terrified. We'll pretend I wasn't nervous as hell

to be left alone with him. Well, technically I wasn't alone with

him; Freddy had woken up and was playing with his cars on the

floor.

"Felix, I don't know what is going on between you and my

daughter but...you need to know something," began Calvin.

"What? You mean that her real name is Princess Morningstar and

that you are – or should I say *were* – Prince Calvin. Why didn't

you tell her? She found out from Eden, erm Hellsolo Eden."

Calvin looked shocked by what I had said. He shot back, "How did

Eden know that Star's true identity is Princess Morningstar?

There are only a few people who know that name."

"Your Father is in Alicade. He is one of the Kings there," I

explained.

Calvin looked away from me and said, in a low voice, "That means

he's dead in this world, doesn't it?"

"Yes, it does. I'm sorry. But that doesn't mean you won't get to

see him again, if that's what you're worried about. I am a mod

avatar, I could pull him through the portal or take you to visit

him," I said. "I found out that witches who have Hellsolo's can end up in Alicade when they die, as well as avatars. I don't know how, but he did it."

I felt like I was rambling on, as I didn't want the subject of Star and I to come back around. But it did, of course. Calvin asked, "So, you and my daughter; are you two an item now?"

"Erm, yes. We made it official not long ago," I said nervously.

"Choose your next words wisely, Felix. What do you mean by 'official'?"

The expression on Calvin's face was one of fury. "What I mean is, we are now girlfriend and boyfriend, that's it," I said, holding out my hands.

"I can't pretend I'm ok with this, but if this is what she wants, I'll have to live with it. All I ask is that you don't break her heart...if you do, I might be forced to break something of yours; and it *won't* be pleasant."

He was joking, right? – I hope – but I gulped nervously, all the same. "I'll try my best not to. I do love her, Mr. Redfield. I promise, I will protect her to the best of my ability."

Calvin reached out his hand and put it on my shoulder. I almost flinched. "Thanks Felix," he said. "One day, when you have children of your own, you'll understand why I'm so protective over mine."

With that, he walked out of the front door. I looked down at Freddy and said, "Well, that was scary."

"That man's scary" Freddy replied, not looking up from his cars.

"Yes, Freddy. Yes, he is. You hungry? Let's go get some food."

That got his attention, sure enough. Freddy jumped into my arms and I took him to the kitchen.

I left Freddy in the kitchen and went to my room to pack a few bits, when there was a knock at the door. "Come in," I called out.

It was Red and Ben. "What do you want?" I asked.

"We just wanted to say thank you, Felix."

"No Ben. It's King Felix," Red said as he backhanded him in the chest.

"Sorry, King Felix," said Ben.

"You know you don't have to call me that," I said.

"Yes. Yes, we do, but you made us avatars. You have given both our lives purpose. We can never thank you enough, and we will always fight with you, King Felix," said Red.

Then they both sank down on to one knee. "Stand up, please," I said; and they did. "Thank you for helping me on this...quest, of sorts; and thanks for your help over in Alicade as well. I really do appreciate all you've done for me."

"When you go back to Alicade will you take us with you?" Ben asked quietly.

I looked at him, then at Red; and then back to Ben. "Is that what you want?" I said.

"No, we want to stay here."

"Good. I don't want you bloody over there with me," I joked.

"You are both avatars now, so you can come and go between the two worlds if you want., I just need to teach you one day how to do it, but for now, I would like you two to stay in the real world to protect the family. Do you think you could both do that?"

"Most definitely King Felix. We will leave you to pack, later King Felix."

"I told you, don't call me that," I said, but they were gone.

I finished packing and was sat in the living room with Freddy, when Star appeared in front of us. She made me jump, but Freddy was fine with it.

"Fix, it's Star," Freddy said, pointing at her.

"I can see that, buddy. I have to go now," I said gently.

"No Fix, Freddy come too?"

"No, not this time. I'll see you in a few days, so don't be sad. Remember, your Prince Freddy now; and Prince's don't cry. I'm King Felix and you don't see me crying, do you? I'll be back in a few days."

"Ok, King Fix," he mumbled sadly.

"How about this, Mini Me: when I get back, we will play whichever game you want to play?"

Freddy nodded his head, very excited at the prospect. He jumped off his chair and ran up the stairs. I watched him as he ran and tripped a few times. I knew full well what he would want us to play; it would be his dinosaur Top Trumps. I swear he cheats; I can never win a game against him. He kicks my butt every time, but still, I am the reigning King of Snap.

Star and I walked into the kitchen, where everyone was still sat talking. Brogue was talking about how there were different universes and about how Kava was from Earth Nova. I probably should have been in there, hearing all about it, but I wanted to be with Freddy for a while.

"Ok, we're leaving now," I said. I wasn't sure how else to say it because I'd always found goodbyes difficult.

"Ok son. Here are the keys to the car and the cabin. Drive safe, Star," said Dad.

"Thanks, Dad. I will see some of you in a few hours."

Mum came over and gave me a kiss on the cheek; and a bag full of food for everyone while we were at the cabin. "Thanks, Mum. I'll see you in a few days."

"Bye my love," she said, trying to hold back tears.

And then we left.

CHAPTER EIGHTEEN

The drive to Lake Halo was easy. There was next to no traffic, it was a Thursday after all, who goes away on a Thursday?

We pulled up at the cabin and Star said, as she got out of the driver's side door, "Wow Felix, this is beautiful. It's a log cabin and it's huge!"

"Are there any other kind of cabins?" I asked, laughing. "So, let me get this right: my Great, Great, Great, Great, Great Granddad built it many, many years ago. It gets inspected every five years or so, just to make sure it's safe to stay in. We haven't ever had any issues with it, even when Great Granddad Felix extended it, like, twenty years ago. Do you want to go inside now?"

"Yes please, lead the way," said Star excitedly.

I grabbed our bags and we went inside. How do I describe the cabin? I don't really know. It's a cabin made out of logs, is that enough? No, ok it's a really big cabin made out of logs.

Once inside, I put the bags on a chair and started telling Star about some of the seats, sofas and tables; which had been in our family for generations. I also grabbed some logs from outside to start a fire. Don't panic; the chimney is made out of stones, so we won't set fire to ourselves. I couldn't get the matches to light and I was getting frustrated.

How the hell am I doing to light the bloody thing? I thought. I stood up; thinking…then I hit myself over the head. I possess power over fire. I clicked my fingers and cupped my hands around the small flame that had appeared in my palm. The fire was easy to start then.

Star, looking around the kitchen, had started to put some of the food away. She turned to me and said, "Felix, there's a fridge in here, but there's electricity running to it."

"Ok, give me a minute. I need to turn on the generator," I said, getting up and going outside to the back of the house, to the shed. I turned all the switches on and pulled the cord. The generator's motor kicked in and started the first time.

When I got back inside, Star wasn't in the kitchen, where she'd been when I went outside. I walked into the living room, looking for her; and found Calvin there. I froze. I really didn't want to be alone with him again, but then Star popped back in with Chadwick in tow. I understood now, Star had started to bring everyone here via teleportation.

She walked over to me and said, "I need a little charge. This is using up a lot of my power, bringing people over here."

"Sure, anything to help out," I replied.

She took my hand and I pushed my energy into her. Once her hair was red, she let go and disappeared. "What was that?" Calvin asked, looking directly at me.

"Being a mod avatar means I possess an energy power; and I can charge Star's power up with mine," I explained.

"That's not a very good idea. She can't be given too much power, or Hellsolo Edan will come out and take her over," Calvin warned.

 "It's fine. Hellsolo Eden and I have a deal, so she won't come out unless she's asked to.

Calvin clearly didn't feel reassured by my answer. He just walked out of the front door, without saying anything else to me.

"It's ok Felix. He'll come around to the idea of you and Star being together eventually. I hear you are official now, so welcome to the family," Chadwick said, as he tapped me on the shoulder and went after his Father.

It took a good few hours for Star to teleport everyone over to the cabin because she had to stop and charge after every jump back here. Star was exhausted, as was I. She had passed out on the sofa after bringing Sean here, but I forced myself to stay awake with the others.

Calvin and Chadwick didn't return until late that evening, but they went straight upstairs to bed. I got Red to show them to their rooms, and I got Ben to show Kava, Brogue and Granddad Felix theirs. I sat down on the sofa, at Star's feet, lent my head back and closed my eyes.

"Felix," said a voice.

"Sean, can this wait? I just need five minutes to recharge my batteries."

"Please Felix," he said.

I could hear the pain in his voice, so I looked up at him, stood up and put my hands on his shoulders. I said "Of course we can talk. What worries you my friend?"

"It's Karl. I'm just concerned about him."

"You don't need to worry. I'll do everything in my power to save him," I assured him.

"I know you will. I suppose I just needed reassuring."

"How about this," I said to him. "I will still give Karl the wind power, but Annadora and Kayos don't know that you have powers now too. You have the wind element as well. How about *you* just concentrate on saving Karl? If he goes in the water, then so do you. You're forgetting that you have just as much power to save him now as I do."

"I hadn't thought of it that way. Thanks Felix."

"Let me ask you one question: why don't you call me 'King Felix', like the others do?"

"Because...I see the look on your face when they call you it. You don't like it very much, do you?"

I took a deep breath and said, "It's not that I don't like it. I love being King and bossing some people around, but you lot are my family and closest friends. I don't want to be treated differently now that now I'm a King."

Sean punched me in the arm (*hard*, let me add) and said, "Not a chance mate! You're still a freak, but you're our freak," he said; and with that, Sean went to bed.

I smiled to myself. I knew Sean would understand me. I looked down at Star, who was still fast asleep. "I should get sleeping beauty to bed," I said to myself. I know they say talking to yourself is the first sign of madness, but you're reading this story…you can't tell me that most of what I'm telling you doesn't sound like madness.

Here we go with another Satan twin's story. When I was 13, they ignored me for the whole month of March. If I spoke to them, they didn't even acknowledge me; or they would walk straight into me and say they got touched by a creepy ghost. I also got into trouble over it as well.

Mum would ask me to tell them that dinner was ready and when I knocked on the door, one of them would open it, look straight passed me, to one side then the other and say, 'It must have been the wind.'

Then, when they were late for dinner, I would get into trouble for 'not telling them'. But then, on the 1st of April, they'd told me it was an April fool's joke. They'd thought it was hilarious.

Back to the here and now.

I gently picked Star up and she nestled her face into my chest. I took her upstairs. When my family and I used to stay at the cabin for the holidays, we created this system that, on the door handle of whichever room you were staying in, you needed to put an 'in use' sign up. The only room left in this part of the cabin (did I tell you this was I big cabin? Like, it's actually huge! My best guess is it's got at least 12 bedrooms. Every few years, the whole family gets together for a family reunion here. That's why it's so big!) is my parent's room.

I took her in there. I used the wind power to flick the bed covers down and gently lay her down and tucked her into bed. I lent down and kissed her forehead; and whispered, "Goodnight, Princess Morningstar."

Star reached out, grabbed my top and said, "Stay with me."

I looked at her for a second, was she talking in her sleep? She still had a hold of my Metallica t-shirt. "Ok," I whispered, and I climbed over her to lie on the other side of the bed.

She wrapped her arms around me and put her head on my chest. I had to focus on steadying my breathing, as she said, "This could be our last night together, one or both of us could die tomorrow.

I didn't want to spend the night alone."

I hugged her tighter and replied, "I know what you mean."

And that's how we fell asleep, just like that.

I don't know what time it was when I got woken up by someone

shouting, "FELIX, GET YOUR HANDS OFF MY DAUGHTER!"

Calvin had shouted so loud, I wouldn't have been surprised if he'd

woken up the whole house. I looked over at Calvin, who was

standing in the doorway. "Mr. Redfield, it's not what it looks like."

"It looks like you've just slept with my daughter?"

"Well technically, yes. But we just slept in the same bed. We

didn't...you know...do anything else."

"Dad, I'm 18 now. I'm an adult, so I can *sleep* with whoever I want

to," Star said, putting extra emphasis on the word sleep, just to

wind Calvin up more. He looked like he was going to have a

stroke.

I glanced sideways at her and thought, *When did you turn 18?*

"You're still 17, young lady. Now Felix, get out of that bed!" Calvin

commanded.

"Star, you turned 18 in Alicade, not here," I whispered as I got out

of the bed.

"Whoops," Star said, sitting up in the bed.

Suddenly, the door flew open; and Chadwick charged in. "Dad is

everything...oh, busted," he said, catching sight of us.

Chadwick burst out laughing. "The pair of you get downstairs, NOW!" Calvin shouted; and stormed out the room, passing a still laughing Chadwick.

"He's going to kill me," I said.

Downstairs, Star and I sat on either side of the sofa with our heads down as Calvin shouted at us for being irresponsible. "But we only slept in the same bed, nothing else happened," I said. I probably should have kept my mouth shut.

Sean walked out of the kitchen with some toast and said, "Yeah, calm down Mr. R. It's not the first time they have slept in the same bed, anyway."

My head snapped up and I looked at Calvin, wide-eyed. "Snitch,' I mouthed at Sean.

"WHAT?" Calvin roared.

"Dad don't stress out. Anyway, you can't say much. How old were you and Mum when you had Kayos?" asked Star.

"We were both 21 and we were married. Do we need to have the… talk?" Calvin said nervously.

Oh my god, please tell me this is *not* happening. He wants to have the sex talk. I wanted the ground to open up and swallow me whole.

"What is going on here?" Granddad Felix said as he walked down the stairs, closely followed by Brogue.

"I've just found Felix and Star in bed together and apparently; they've been sleeping together for a while."

"Yes, *sleeping* being the operative word. That's it, nothing else," I said hurriedly, as I stood up.

Calvin glared at me and I sat back down. "Mr. Redfield, for starters, you will address these two by their correct titles: King Felix and Princess Morningstar. Secondly, you will *never* raise your voice to the King like that again. It's very insulting," said Granddad Felix, standing next to the sofa with his arms crossed over his chest.

"Mr. Redfield," Brogue continued. "You may not be from Alicade or the Arcana, nor are you an avatar, but you are on a King's quest. He is your superior in this regard; and what he does with Princess Morningstar is, frankly, none of your damn business."

Way to poke the bear, Brogue, I thought, as Calvin shouted, "She is my *daughter*!"

I stood back up and said, "Come on gents, let's cool it for a moment. Star and I have only been going out officially for a few weeks – or days in real-world time. Whichever way you choose to look at it is fine, from here or from Alicade. Yes, we may occasionally sleep in the same bed, but that's it, I swear. We want to be together and I'm sorry Calvin, but there's nothing you can do about it. As long as Star chooses to be with me, I'm not going anywhere. I will always want to be with Star and only her. And, one day in the future, I hope she will be my Queen."

Every word was heartfelt, and every word was true. I could see in Calvin's face that he now understood. I suppose it would hard for him to let go of her. I felt something in my hand then.

Star had gotten up of the sofa and grabbed my hand. As she did so, she said, "And I will *always* want to be with Felix. I'm sorry Dad." He looked sad, but just nodded in agreement.

"Now that all that drama is over, we need to talk about where we are going to start looking for Annadora and Kayos," I said, glad to finally be off the topic of mine and Star's relationship.

"Chadwick mentioned the pond that you spoke about yesterday," said Calvin. "Apparently, it's about a half mile west from here. Chadwick and I checked it out last night; and it's the one in his vision."

"I don't suppose you know what kind of time it will all be happening?" I asked Chadwick."I don't, sorry," Chadwick responded. "All I know is that Annadora and Kayos came out of hiding when Ben and Red arrive at the little pond."

"Ok, thanks. Sean, could you go and wake the twins up, please? They should be here for this too."

"Will do," he said; and off he went to get them.

"We all need to go to the pond to look for vantage points and weaknesses in our position," I said. We all have different powers –"

"Hang on, stop the boat," Chadwick interrupted, turning to Star. "I was still half asleep. I've just realised, they've been calling you Princess Morningstar? What the hell?"

I cut back in, saying, "Chadwick, I will explain everything to you later, but first we need –"

I was cut short again when there was a huge bang from upstairs; and we heard Sean shout, "Stay in bed then, see if I care!" Sean stomped down the stairs. "They told me that they are not getting out of bed; and they told me to do one."

"Oh, really?" I said. Letting go of Star's hand, I gave her a quick kiss on the cheek. "Won't get out of bed, you say?"

I ran up the stairs two at a time. The twins were in the room they always used when we stayed her, the one with their 'Enter and Die' sign on the door. *This is going to be fun,* I thought to myself. I kicked the door so hard it flew open and hit the wall. It swung open with so much force that one of its hinges came loose. I booted it so that hard I'm surprised my foot didn't go straight through it.

"WHAT DO YOU TWO THINK YOU ARE PLAYING AT?" I boomed, my voice echoing through the room loudly. "I gave Sean a command to come and get you, and you, lazy *shits* disobey my order! Don't make me regret bringing you two along and making you avatars. Be downstairs in five minutes. If you're not then I will get Star to take you home, minus your powers. Get up, NOW!"

They both jumped out of bed and were on their knees in front of me in a second, their heads almost touching the floor. "We are sorry, my King. We won't disobey you again," Ben grovelled.

"Yes, my King, we are sorry," Red wailed.

Having the twins grovelling at my feet was a fantastic feeling.

"Five minutes," I barked, then I left their room.

They were downstairs in three minutes and 39 seconds, I timed them. "Well done, so you can take orders," I said sarcastically, before turning to everyone. "So, the plan is we go to the pond in an hour to look at it; and plan out our attack."

I picked up mine and Star's bags, which Calvin wasn't too happy about, but he didn't protest. I went to our room and got changed. Star got changed in the bathroom.

When she came out, she looked so good. She had on a pair of denim shorts and a Panic! at the Disco t-shirt. The t-shirt was tied into a knot on Star's left-hand side. She had a pair of black Doc Martens on her feet.,

"Hang on a second, that's my top," I said; and Star just smiled. She started slowly walking over to me. "What, this old thing? No, it's mine," she said.

"I'm not too sure it is," I said, putting my hands on her hips and pulling her closer.

"It's definitely mine," she said.

"Ok, so if it's yours, then how did you get this hole in it?" I asked, putting my finger in the hole and touching her exposed skin on the right side.

"Oh no, King Felix, you ripped my top," she said jokingly.

"I'm ever so sorry, Princess Morningstar," I replied, exaggeratedly. "It's just that it looks exactly like a top I have – or had – over in Alicade; and it had a hole in the exact same place. It's where I was stabbed when I was fighting."

"You got stabbed?" Star said, suddenly serious.

"Yeah, it was when I got stuck over there. It was really bad too. If it had been an inch to the right, it could have been fatal."

"Oh my god, I don't remember seeing a scar on you," she said.

"You won't have done. My body was still here, untouched – buried, but untouched. None of my old battle scars exist since I came back here. I was untouched by time too," I explained.

"So, you're still only 16. Does that mean I'm dating a younger man?" she asked; a smile in her voice.

"Well technically, in Alicade, I'm about 25."

"Wow, an older man then," Star said, wrapping her arms around my neck and kissing me.

I didn't want to let her go, but all good things must come to an end. There was a knock at the door. "Sorry to disturb you, King Felix, but we are all ready to go," said Ben.

"We'll be there in a minute," I said, as I looked deep into Star's eyes.

I tried to make my body move, but I was frozen to the spot. I was starting to panic, now that the time had finally come to face Annadora and Kayos. Today was the day that Karl was supposed to die.

I looked back at Star and said, "Star, do you think Chadwick's vision could have changed?"

"Why do you ask?" she questioned.

"When I asked him last time, when Kava was here; there was no change. But now, we have three more people with us, one of them being your Father who wasn't in Chadwick's vision."

"I don't know Felix, ask him."

"I think I will."

I leant down, kissed her again; and said, "Come on, before they send Calvin in to get us."

Star laughed as we left the room.

I asked Chadwick to stay behind with Ben and Red and to check whether anything in his vision has changed, which he agreed to do. The twins were not so happy with this arrangement. They

didn't want to be on babysitting duties, but it was their
punishment for this morning.

It didn't take long to get to the pond.

Calvin was talking to Granddad Felix about tactics when we got
there. I'm pretty sure he should've been talking to me about it,
but I didn't say anything, and I let it slide. I'll bet he's still not too
happy with Star and I, after this morning, Oh well.

"Sean, I want you to *only* look out of Karl," I instructed him. "If he
moves, you move. I'll get Ben to cover you. Star…"

"I know, Hellsolo Eden needs to come out to play," she said,
kicking a stone into the pond.

I walked over to her and tilted her face up, so that she was
looking at me. "I know it's going to be hard for you and your
family, fighting with your Mother and Kayos, but yes, Eden needs
to come out," I said, giving her a gentle kiss.

"Hey, Ben and Red are back," said Sean.

My stomach sank. Chadwick had told me that, in his vision, Kayos
and Annadora appear as soon as Red and Ben have arrived at the
pond. *This is it,* I thought. The battle starts now. I quickly pulled
away from Star and shouted, "THEY'RE HERE, PLACES
EVERYONE!"

Not that anyone really knew where to stand. We hadn't had time
to go over everything properly yet. I frantically looked around,
but I couldn't see any sign of Annadora, Kayos or Karl. No wait,

there, at the other side of the pond – there they were. And they weren't alone. There must have been about twenty people walking behind them, but there was still no sign of Karl.

"Well," said Annadora as she approached. "I have to say I'm impressed, darling Felix. You figured out that I was lying about Drake Forest. How did you find out?"

"It was all thanks to Chadwick," I replied. "I gave him back his foresight." I looked around for him, but I couldn't see him anywhere. *Where the hell is, he?* I thought to myself.

"Well done, Felix," said Kayos sarcastically.

"Actually, it's *King Felix* now," I said. "I'm the new King of the Arcana. I am now your King, Annadora. I order you stop this now, before it goes too far."

"Where's Karl?" Sean interrupted.

Kayos walked into the crowd of people that had shown up with him and Annadora. When he re-emerged, he had Karl by the neck. Sean and I both took a step forward. "Stay where you are, *King* Felix, or little Karl here dies!" Kayos cried, squeezing Karl's neck tighter.

Karl clawed at Kayos hand to loosen it, but he couldn't., "Ok, ok, Sean stand back," I told him.

"Do you have my item?" Annadora asked, walking over to the edge of the pond.

"Stand down Anna, it doesn't have to be this way," Calvin said, walking past me.

"Mr. Redfield, what are you doing?" I said, in a warning tone.

Calvin turned to me and said, "I'm buying you some time, my King."

"Felix, give Karl the power now while they're talking," whispered Sean.

I nodded. I closed my eyes to try and tune out all the talking. I let my wind power fill me up from the inside. Round and round it flowed. Then I split it in half, as I'd done when I'd turned some of the other into avatars. I opened my eyes and looked straight at Karl. I eased the wind power – housed in an energy bubble – over the pond.

"Felix is –?" I held my hand up to silence Sean, I needed to concentrate.

My breathing started to get heavier. I had never pushed a power so far out of my body. All it wanted to do was spring back into me, but I pushed on. I was getting lightheaded by the time the power had reached Karl.

Karl's body started to shake and Kayos noticed. He looked over at me and said, "Hey, what are you doing to Karl?"

I fell to my knees and snapped, "Nothing," as my eyes rolled back and I passed out.

I must have only been out for a few minutes, because when I came to everyone was in the same place as before, but just a bit closer to me.

"Did you have a nice nap?" Kayos shouted across to me still gripping on to Karl.

"No, not really," I said back.

"ENOUGH! Where is my Crybecker?" Annadora screamed, getting angry.

I shakily got to my feet and walked to the edge of the pond. I put my hand in my jeans pocket and pulled out the stone.

"Give it to me!" she demanded.

"Not until you release Karl," I said calmly.

"Not a chance, the stone first," Kayos said.

"Sean, get ready," I whispered, he nodded.

"Felix, don't do anything stupid," Star whispered.

"You want it, Annadora? Go and get it," I said; and I threw it into the pond. As soon as the Crybecker hit the water, I used my water possession to turn the pond into a whirlpool.

"NO!" Annadora screamed.

Kayos turned to me and said, "Say goodbye to your friend."

And with that, Kayos pushed Karl into the water. "Sean, NOW!" I bellowed.

Sean jumped into the water after Karl, just as the small army

Annadora had brought with her charged us. "Protect the King!"

Brogue shouted.

"No, go and get Annadora," I commanded.

"Hellsolo Eden," I heard Star say.

A split second later, I heard worse, as Calvin said, "Hellsolo Blood

wolf!"

"Calvin, NO!" I shouted, but it was too late. His eyes were already

turning blood red. *Crap,* I thought.

Before I knew what was happening, there was a fireball heading

my way. Just in time, someone pushed me out its path. It was

Chadwick. "Where the *hell* have you been?" I said, as another one

of Annadora's men rushed at us.

I punched our attacker in the face and Chadwick swiped his legs

out from under him. "When we were walking back, I had a vision.

It was strange...I've never had a vision out of the blue like that.

I've always been able to control when I get one."

Before I could ask Chadwick anything more about the vision, Sean

caught my eye. He was crawling out of the water, with Karl

behind him. They lay on the floor, coughing. I fought my way over

to them. I took out four of Annadora's men along the way, with

Chadwick's help.

"Karl," I said, dropping to my knees and hugging him too tightly.

"King Felix, we need to move," Chadwick said, as he took another guy out.

Chadwick has no avatar powers, nor has he got magic, but he is still nifty in a fight. "Sean, get Karl back to the cabin, we will be there as soon as we can," I said hurriedly.

"Yes ok. Come on, Karl," Sean said, helping Karl up.

I cleared a path for them by using my wind power to push everyone out the way. I accidentally pushed Red away too. "HEY! Watch where you're aiming," shouted Red, quickly adding "my King" when he saw that it was me who'd hit him.

"Ouch, that really hurt," he said as he stood back up.

"Go now," I said. We protected them until they were out of sight.

"Chadwick, I need to go find Annadora," I told him.

"Please, don't hurt her. I know she's done some bad things, but she's still my Mother."

I put my hand on his shoulder and said, "I'll try. I just want to stop her from doing what she's trying to do. I need to take her to Falkor. You know as well as I do that's where she ends up being held."

Chadwick nodded his understanding, "Thanks, King Felix."

I searched all around for her, but she was nowhere to be seen. I left the fighting to go and look for her. A little way into the forest, I found someone else instead. "Kayos," I said to myself.

"Felix, Felix, Felix...we meet alone, again," he replied.

"Where is Annadora?" I asked him.

"Gone," he said simply.

"Gone where?"

"When you threw her Crybecker into the water she couldn't find it, she went AWOL and left."

"Who said I *actually* threw her Crybecker into the water? Could you really see what it looked like from all the way over where you were standing? Because I'm 99.99% sure it's still in my pocket."

"You're lying," he spat.

"Am I?" I said, as I pulled the real Crybecker out of my back pocket.

"Give it to me and I'll leave without hurting anyone," Kayos said, taking a step forward.

"Not a chance," I said, echoing what he had said to me earlier. I put the Crybecker back in my pocket. "Kayos, you have to see that she's just using you to get what she wants."

He didn't say anything, so I went on, "She just wants to destroy everything. Do you not feel anything for your Dad, brother or sister? She's isolated you from them. Your Mother turned Star's Hellsolo evil and made Star hurt Chadwick."

Kayos was getting uncomfortable. "Shut up, Felix! You don't know anything; you just want to kill her!"

"No, I don't. That's what Aries told me I had to do, but I gave Chadwick his foresight back; and he told me I don't kill her and that she gets taken to Falkor."

"As a prisoner, I don't think so," Kayos said. Then he said something in Latin and reached out his right hand. It looked like he'd grabbed something from thin air and pulled it in front of him.

I was unsure what he'd done, until a tree trunk came hurtling towards me. I couldn't move quickly enough. The tree trunk slammed into me hard. *Wow that hurt*! Before I could get up, Kayos ran over to me and kicked me in the stomach; then in the face.

"Ahhhh," I shouted, crying out in pain.

Kayos went for my pocket, but I grabbed his hand and let the fire set my arm alight. He pulled away from me and put out the flames that were climbing up his sleeve.

"You shouldn't take things that don't belong to you, Felix," he shouted.

"It's not yours," I shot back. "It's from Alicade, where I am King, so that makes it mine by default." I got up and charged him. I rugby tackled him to the ground, and we wrestled for a few minutes. I landed a few punches, but Kayos landed more.

He pushed me off him and got up, saying, "Thanks for this." He was rolling Annadora's Crybecker around in his fingers.

"NO!" I shouted.

I got up and jumped on his back, wrapping my arm around his throat, so that his neck was in the crease of my elbow. I started to squeeze his neck and pull his energy out of him as fast as I could. I couldn't let him go with the Crybecker.

I whispered in his ear, "I told Chadwick I wouldn't hurt your Mother, but he didn't say I couldn't hurt you."

I knew Kayos' energy was nearly all gone. "Kill me. I will *never* tell you where she is," he said as he fell to his knees.

I kept my hold on his throat as he fell, rolling onto my back. "Killing you would be too easy," I said; and then he fell unconscious.

Holy crap! I could feel his Hellsolo power. It felt just like Calvin's/Hellsolo Blood wolf's energy. I rolled Kayos off me and got the Crybecker out of his hand, while putting it back into my pocket I tried so hard not to pass out, but I did.

CHAPTER NINETEEN

When I woke up, I could see it was dark outside through the bedroom window.

Star was curled up beside me, fast asleep. I stayed there for a while, just watching her sleep. Creepy, I know, but hey, she's my girlfriend. I'm allowed to do it. I kissed her forehead and slid out of bed.

The cabin was so quiet. *Has everyone else gone home? I thought.*

There was a light on downstairs. It looked to be coming from the kitchen, so I headed there.

When I walked into the kitchen, Karl was sat at the table. "Hey Felix, you're awake," he said in greeting.

"Yeah, how long was I out for this time?" I asked.

"Two days, it's early hours Monday morning."

"Two days! Crap, I bet everyone was worried?"

"We were at first, but you were breathing, so we knew you would wake up eventually. How do you feel?" Karl asked, taking a bite of his sandwich.

My belly growled at the sight. "Would you like some?" Karl asked.

"Yes please," I replied, sitting down opposite him.

Karl handed me half of his sandwich. I've never really been a tuna fan, but this tasted divine. "So, how are you feeling?" Karl repeated his question.

"I feel like crap…but I feel energized at the same time. I can still feel Kayos' Hellsolo power in me. It's like it was supercharged or something."

"You must have drained every last drop of energy he had. Kayos still hasn't woken up either."

"Kayos is here too?" I asked, alarmed.

"Yes. When we found you, you and Kayos had both passed out. Star had to fix your face because your jaw was broken."

I felt my jaw automatically, but it was as good as new. "Yes, that's where Kayos kicked me."

Karl went on, "Anyway, he's in the other part of the cabin. I think Sean is on guard duty tonight. So, has a lot changed since I've been gone?"

I ignored his question; I was more worried about what he may have suffered at Annadora and Kayos' hands. "Did they mistreat you? I will kill them if they did."

"No, quite the opposite," Karl said. "I was expecting them to torture me or something, but it was odd. They made sure I had food and drink. They actually treated me better than I get treated at home."

Karl hasn't had the best life. When I got blown out that tree when I was younger and died for five minutes, it messed up his head. He had to go to a psychologist; and that was about the time when his Dad started to beat him for not being strong enough to cope. His Mother hadn't cared about what was happening to him. She just liked to drink herself to sleep, still does in fact. When it got too bad at home, Karl would come and stay at my house. Karl never really stayed at Sean's, because Sean's Dad asked too many questions. The only saving grace was Karl's older brother, Nick. But he wasn't always at home to protect Karl.

"Well, I'm glad you're back," I said, finishing off my half of Karl's sandwich.

"I am too. Thanks, King Felix," he said and smiled.

"So, they told you about that then?"

"Yes, they filled me in on everything I've missed," he chuckled and started counting things off on his fingers. "You're a King, Star is a Princess, Chadwick is a Prince – as is Freddy, nice one by the way. You and Star are finally official, thank god. Oh, and you made Sean, Ben and Red avatars. You even went against my wishes and made me an avatar too. Have I missed anything?"

"I'm sorry Karl, but I had to do something. I couldn't just let you drown, could I? I can take your power back if you want?" I told him.

"No, it's fine. I've gotten used to it now," Karl said, making a wind orb in his hand.

We stayed in the kitchen, talking until it started getting light out. Karl told me that Chadwick had taken Calvin home in the car. Apparently, Calvin had been a wreck after fighting with his Hellsolo and taking back control of his body. He also didn't know that we have Kayos. Everyone thought it best to keep it from him, with the current state he was in. No one else had wanted to leave with them; they all wanted to stay here with me.

"King Felix, finally awake," Kava said, walking into the kitchen.

"Yes, finally," I smiled. "Why are you up so early?"

"I've got the next watch at six...on Kayos. I'm starving. Now that you're awake, does that mean we can go back to your house, back to your Mum's cooking?"

"Soon, not long now," I laughed.

We stayed in the cabin a few more days so that I had time to build up my strength. I got Star to take the twins home to protect the family. Annadora was still out there; and she was alone now, so god only knows what she would do next. Between the seven of us, we watched over Kayos while he slept. I could feel his energy coming back, but really, really slowly.

The day finally came when I was strong enough to walk more than 50 feet without needing to rest or pass out. Granddad Felix led the way. I got Sean and Karl to stay behind to watch Kayos.

His energy wasn't even back at half strength yet, so it was most likely he wouldn't wake up anytime soon.

We walked for what felt like hours, until I said, "I needed a rest. How do you do this all the time, old man?" I joked with my Granddad, as I sat down on the floor. I still wasn't feeling 100% well.

"Star, what's Kayos' Hellsolo called?" I asked, trying to distract myself from how exhausted I felt.

"Hellsolo Pax, but you will never see him. Kayos has more than enough power in him to control his Hellsolo. Hellsolo Pax has the most beautiful purple eyes."

"How is Kayos so strong?" I said, thinking out loud.

"Kayos took Hellsolo Pax's power into himself," Star said. "And now, he controls that power completely."

"Wow, that's messed up," I breathed.

"Come on my King, there's not far to go," Granddad Felix said. I nodded at him as Star helped me up off the floor.

We walked for about 20 more minutes until we came upon the crypt, it looked so out of place being in the middle of the woods. It was Balthazar's crypt. This is what we'd been searching for. It looked just like a crypt from the olden days, where you would bury generations of a family. It was huge.

When walking up to it I noticed it was covered in stone carvings of angels and goblins. "Wow, this looks amazing," Star said, as she reached up to touch an angel's foot.

"It was built a very long time a long time ago, just for the sole purpose of holding evil beings," Brogue said, walking passed us. We both followed him around the corner. We could see a huge hole where the door should have been. The big stone door was broken into pieces on the floor. "I'm guessing that's not a good sign?" I asked as Granddad Felix ran to the door.

"No, it isn't, King Felix," my Granddad said, his face ashen. "He's gone...Baltazar is free."

To Be Continued……

First and foremost, I would like to thank everyone for their kind words and their encouragements for me to carry on writing, and them bombarding me with messages for this book to come out this has encouraged me to continue putting my imagination in writing.

I would like to say a huge thank you to Shane Millar for editing and proofreading this book for me, he has done an amazing job, better than I could have imagined, I hope to work with him more in the future.

I hope you all enjoyed reading the series so far, I've loved to be able to continue to bring Felix's story to life.

It would be amazing if you would take the time to follow me, also please leave feedback it would be great to read what you think of my book.

Facebook: https://www.facebook.com/carlaannpearson/
Twitter: https://twitter.com/Carla_A_Pearson
Instagram: https://www.instagram.com/carla_a_pearson/
Goodreads: https://www.goodreads.com/user/show/88276668-carla-pearson

Much Love x